Mack Bolan applauds ABLE TEAM:

"**Carl Lyons** is Mr. Ironman—a hard-punching hotshot, yes, but steel-bound to his country. Lyons and his assault rifle are my odds-on favorites for kicking hell in the butt.

"**Pol Blancanales** has the kind of combat wisdom that is sure to keep the dicks on the run. I value Pol's maturity—I count it vital to the survival of the world.

"**Gadgets Schwarz** is a hellfire brother whose killing quests are conducted with hi-tech wizardry and guts. These men are my weapons of justice. Watch out."

"Written in the inimitable Executioner style!"
—*Mystery News*

D0424571

Other books you will enjoy
in Gold Eagle's Executioner series

MACK BOLAN
The Executioner

Mack Bolan's
PHOENIX FORCE

Amazon Slaughter

Dick Stivers

A GOLD EAGLE BOOK FROM

TORONTO · NEW YORK · LONDON

First edition March 1983

ISBN 0-373-61204-4

Special thanks and acknowledgment to
C.J. Shiao for his contributions to this work.

Printed in Canada

1

Screams came from the radio, then only electronic hiss.

"Stop! Stop the truck!" Abbott shouted, his gaunt, heroin-ravaged face twisted with panic. He switched frequencies on his hand radio, praying for an answer from the control room. Then he realized the truck had not slowed. Like a scene from a nightmare, the truck continued forward. Only a hundred yards separated him from the atomic reactor complex.

"Stop!" Abbott shouted again, grabbing for the steering wheel. The squat, jowly driver stared at him, uncomprehendingly. Abbott repeated the command in Portuguese. The driver hit the brakes.

Dust swirled around the Renault military truck. In front of them, at the end of the dirt-and-gravel corridor cut through the jungle, the gray hemisphere of the reactor's containment vessel rose from the raw red earth. The gray rectangles of the other buildings clustered around the dome. Soaring mahogany and mapacu and rubber trees overhung the area, branches and shadows camouflaging the reactor complex from airborne observation.

Staring at the reactor dome, Abbott felt sweat flow down his body. The radio hissed with static. Abbott knew what the screams meant, and the electronic hiss. But he still watched the dome, hoping to hell that the concrete could contain the atomic and chemical horror that raged inside.

"Mr. Abbott." A voice startled him. He turned, saw one of the work-gang overseers approaching the truck. The overseer wore a pith helmet and olive drab green shorts. His bronzed torso and legs streamed sweat. He crossed his hands over the shotgun hanging by its sling from his shoulder.

"I need a truck to get those Indians back to the compound." The overseer stepped up on the Renault's bumper. He glanced to the reactor buildings. "I buzzed the Unit for a truck, but my walkie-talkie isn't working right."

The Renault lurched, rocked on its springs. Dense white smoke billowed from the complex. The earth shuddered mightily as the reinforced concrete walls of the turbine building collapsed outward, jagged sections twisting as they fell. Clouds of white smoke churned into the sky. Then the scene shimmered as waves of heat poured from the gaping holes. The jungle trees overhanging the reactor complex burst into flames.

"Get us out of here!" Abbott heard himself shouting in English and Portuguese and Spanish, as he watched the nuclear catastrophe.

Grinding the gears, the driver threw the transmission into reverse, sped backward. The overseer clung to the side mirror as the truck bounced. The truck swerved into a wide backward turn.

An Indian screamed as he died under the wheels. The other Indians dropped their shovels and ran as fast as their ankle chains allowed. The truck driver did not pause as he threw the truck into first gear and accelerated.

Abbott shouted into the hand radio, "Explosion at Unit One! Evacuate all work areas. Get our people into the shelters. Issue the oxygen and the anticontamination suits. Turn on the sirens right now and get—''

"Shut up!" a command blared from the radio. "What's going on there? We only see some smoke—"

"You idiot! That's radioactive sodium hydroxide. That's gaseous lye. Anybody who breathes that dies! Anyone it touches is contaminated."

"Is that Mr. Abbott?" the voice asked.

"Yes, this is Abbott. Unit One's exploding. The core could go any second. That's plutonium! You understand? Plutonium!"

"Yes, sir. Doing it right away. The alarms...."

Switching off his hand radio, Abbott leaned from the truck's window to look back. Swirling red road dust obscured his view of the reactor dome. But above the narrow slash through the jungle, he saw the billowing white cloud of caustic sodium hydroxide. Flames and black smoke leaped from the burning jungle. But he heard no more explosions.

He faced forward again and shouted at the Brazilian driver to go faster. Hurtling over the road, Abbott closed his eyes, visualized the destruction inside the complex, the burning metallic sodium, the hydrogen fires, the technicians cremated alive. He knew that as the seconds and minutes passed without the flowing sodium coolant, the temperature of the uranium and plutonium fuel core would rise. If the fuel melted, if the isotopes and transuranium elements fused, if the metals went critical and he remained within a mile of the complex, he would never feel the flash that vaporized him. Only distance could save him.

George Abbott, scientist-turned-addict-turned-pirate atomic physicist, shivered with the knowledge of his certain death. He might die in the next minute, the atomic flash reducing him to ash and superheated vapor and charged particles. Or he would die in months or years, destroyed by the cancers eating his body. But his death was certain.

Death by nuclear explosion. Death by plutonium cancer. Death.

2

On the video projection screen, the white of a storm a thousand miles wide swirled over the Atlantic Ocean and the coast of Brazil. Hundreds of miles into the continent, as the vast, river-veined geography turned beneath the satellite camera, the storm feathered to specks that left another thousand miles of Amazon jungle under a cloudless tropical sky. Sunlight flashed from a twenty-mile-wide tributary of the river.

Raising his voice over the whine of the air force jet's engines, Hal Brognola, Mack Bolan's chief liaison officer for the president's secret antiterrorist force known as Stony Man, touched a pointer to the video screen.

"Notice this one cloud," he said, pointing to a smear of white several hundred miles east of the snow-crowned Andes. No other clouds marked that expanse of green.

"Spectrographic analysis revealed it wasn't water vapor." Brognola pressed a control button. The natural greens and blues disappeared, replaced by phosphorescent reds, blues, purples. "This is computer-enhanced videography. Notice that little cloud now...."

The one point glowed brilliant yellow. As Brognola was speaking, the yellow point had expanded, the camera zooming in until the yellow smear, now streaked and dappled with orange and red, filled the screen. Brognola pointed to the white center.

"Right there, 1000° Fahrenheit. The National Security Agency parked the satellite over this hot spot, monitored it. . . ."

The three men of Able Team were leaning back in their leather-upholstered chairs and glancing at the maps of Brazil they held. Gadgets Schwarz interrupted.

"What was the spectroanalysis?"

"Sodium oxides. Principally sodium hydroxide. Now the photos."

Gadgets stammered, blurted out: "Man, that. . . it. . . those oxides could only. . . . Oh, shit. That's got to be wrong. That means—"

"It was radioactive. . . ."

"Radioactive?" Carl Lyons asked. "Like atomic?"

Brognola pressed the remote control again. Black-and-white images filled the screen. With the pointer, he traced a line across the mottled ground. A break in the jungle showed here and there along it. The breaks suggested a road.

"Did the Brazilians test a bomb or something?" Rosario Blancanales asked. "Or is that Bolivian territory?"

"Not a bomb," Gadgets answered, his voice quiet.

"The site appears to be in Brazil, but only just. It's only a few miles from territory that Bolivia claims," said Hal.

"How much radioactivity?" Gadgets asked.

"What is this, a guessing game?" Lyons demanded. "Was it a bomb or not?"

"A bomb factory," Gadgets answered. "How much radioactivity, Hal?"

"We don't know. . . ."

"A bomb factory?" Lyons asked. "What was it that happened? A nuke went off?"

"What about local people?" Blancanales broke in. "Any information on what happened to them?"

"And who set up the factory?" Lyons pressed. "The Brazilians? I didn't know they had the—"

"Gentlemen," Brognola smiled. "If we knew the answers to these questions, you three men would not be en route to the Amazon. Allow me to return to the briefing. A spy satellite has given us a few photos, but not much...."

Indicating roads and clearings and structures with the pointer, Brognola flashed a series of grainy blowups on the video screen. "They seem to have gone through the jungle in such a way as to maximize their overhead cover. If we hadn't spotted the sodium hydroxide and the heat, we couldn't have found the installation.

"When Schwarz described the setup as a bomb factory, he was not entirely correct, I think. What we believe they're manufacturing is plutonium."

"But they could take the plutonium to make a bomb," Gadgets added. "Every terrorist, every fanatic in the world has got the how-to books, but none of them has the plutonium. Yet."

"It could be that this group—" Brognola nodded, tapping the satellite photo on the screen "—has the technology and financing to take the next logical step—or insane step—and fabricate nuclear weapons."

"But how do we know they can make plutonium?" Blancanales countered. "All we've got are those satellite photos."

"It's the sodium hydroxide, Rosario," muttered Gadgets. "It means a whole lot of sodium hit the environment. And the only reason to have that much metallic sodium in one place is a plutonium breeder reactor. A plutonium breeder uses liquid metallic sodium as a coolant. Most reactors use water as a coolant. The water flows around the core, draws off the heat and becomes steam. The steam runs the turbines to make electrical power. But a breeder needs sodium coolant, both to cool it and to moderate the plutonium fission process. Keeps it from going 'boom.' The sodium surrounds and cools the core. It keeps the rate of reaction down. Then it goes through a heat exchanger to heat up the water. The steam makes electrical power. And as a by-product, instead of a pile of used-up uranium 235, you've got more plutonium than you started with.''

''Could this be some kind of supersecret Brazilian power plant?'' Lyons asked. ''I mean, the government there isn't going to let a gang of crazies set up a nuke factory.''

''There is no government where you're going,'' Brognola answered. ''No roads, no towns, nothing. All the maps are approximate. What information we have mentions headhunters and cannibals.''

''Is there no other explanation for what the satellite pictures show?'' Blancanales asked.

''That's why you three are going!'' A voice boomed from the back of the plane. Andrez Konzaki, the Stony Man weaponsmith, was seated behind a conference table. ''Why don't you let Hal finish your briefing? Both of us have to get off in Miami, and I need to talk to you, too. That gives us thirty-five minutes more. No more wasting time, hey?''

Lyons gave the ex-marine a quick salute. ''Yes, sir! No more questions from me.''

Brognola dropped a thick folder of maps and photocopies in front of each member of Able Team. ''The briefing on the satellite intelligence is over. Here's miscellaneous information on the region. The Indians, the land, the natural hazards. Radiation hazards and decontamination procedures. This jet will take you to an airfield in Peru. You'll transfer to a DC-3 for the hop over the Andes. Our CIA liaison has arranged a team of Indians to take you into the area.

"You'll carry very basic antiradiation gear. Remember, your assignment is only to gather information. If the area is radioactive, you will withdraw. We'll have a satellite directly over your area of operation. Schwarz will have an instantaneous link to Stony Man. As the situation evolves, your mission directive may change. They're yours, Andrez. We have twenty-nine minutes before Miami."

Lyons went to the back of the executive jet's luxurious compartment, where the square-shouldered, bull-necked Konzaki had spread equipment over the conference table. "Now we start on the important stuff. What've you got for us?"

"Standard weapons...."

"The Atchisson! All right! Are the bugs worked out yet?"

"It wouldn't be going with you otherwise."

Lyons picked up the black-metal-and-plastic assault shotgun. Looking like an oversize M-16, the selective-fire shotgun chambered both standard and Magnum 12-gauge shot shells from a 7-round box magazine or a 20-round drum magazine.

"What is that monster?" Gadgets asked.

"That's the LCKD," Konzaki told him. "Short for 'Lyons's Crowd-Killing Device.' Just a joke, guys. It's an Atchisson Assault 12. It'll be on the market soon. I remanufactured the pressings in titanium to bring down the weight. Added the carrying handle, M-16 style."

"Who's carrying the ammunition for that thing?" Blancanales asked. "Looks like it could go through a hundred rounds a minute."

"It could," Konzaki answered. "But the forestock's plastic would burst into flames. I packed twelve magazines of double-ought and number two shot mix. The British developed that mix in Malaysia; it works great in the jungle. And two magazines of one-ounce rifled slugs with Kevlar-defeating steel dart cores.''

"How much does all of that weigh?" Blancanales pressed.

"It's mine," Lyons told his teammates. "I'll carry it. You two take those Matty Mattels." He pointed to the rifles on the table, a CAR-15 and an M-16/M-203 over-and-under assault rifle/grenade launcher.

"Yeah, you'll carry the monster," Gadgets joked, "but who'll carry you? And what happens if there's more than one firefight? You'll be out of ammunition."

Konzaki answered for Lyons. "The Agency files noted that 12-gauge shotguns are the most common hunting weapons in Brazil and Bolivia. There will be ammunition available. But I don't think you'll need it. Consider the numbers. I hand-packed the shot rounds. By cutting the wadding and using Magnum cases with a standard charge of powder, I got eight double-oughts and fifty number twos into each round. On full auto, Lyons can put out more than four hundred pellets in one and a half seconds. You get ambushed, that weapon can get you out. There it is.''

"Fire superiority," Lyons grinned.

"Okay," Blancanales agreed, "but you carry it. What goes on with these rifles? Anything special?"

"Luminous night-sights, titanium weight reduction, selective-fire sears—one-shot, three-shot, or full auto," Konzaki said, turning to the field rifles. "And they have barrels bored for the new NATO slug—one twist in seven inches instead of the old one-in-twelve. It'll give you better accuracy at extreme ranges, less wind drift and enhanced flesh-destroying characteristics."

"Tell us more," Blancanales said.

"Well, you know all about what happens when a 5.56mm slug hits a body. The new NATO slug spins almost twice as fast. And it has more weight. Sixty-five grains instead of the old forty-grain weight. The NATO slug also has a steel core. It will defeat all soft body armor. I loaded the magazines with steel cores and hunting slugs. Every other round is a hollowpoint."

"No Geneva Convention where we're going," Lyons commented.

Konzaki glanced at his watch, continued. "And each one of you will have a Beretta 93-R."

He pointed to three web belts carrying holsters and magazine pouches. Blancanales unsnapped a holster flap, slipped out the Parkerized-black pistol. Representing the cutting edge of Beretta's technology, the auto-pistol featured semi-auto or three-shot bursts. An oversize trigger guard and a fold-down grip provided for a two-handed hold. Fitted with a suppressor and firing custom-loaded 9mm cartridges, it killed without a sound.

"We had some problems with that subsonic ammunition," Blancanales told Konzaki. "I had to shoot one biker five times to drop him."

"Yes. You told me. So I flew out to the Coast for the autopsies on the Outlaws. Of the three slugs in the chest of that creep, one went through his wallet and lodged in rib cartilage. The other two shattered ribs, passed through his lungs and lodged against the back of his rib cage. Though he was definitely out of the action, I considered that substandard performance. Now the subsonics have steel cores. The steel cores do nothing for the shock power, but they have superior penetration characteristics. You can expect through-and-through torso wounds on your targets. But just barely. Ultimately, accuracy is the determining factor."

Lyons opened his jacket to touch his Colt Python. "I'm taking my Magnum. Those little Italian toys make me nervous."

"Whatever's appropriate, Mr. Lyons. Different weapons for different situations."

They felt the jet bank into a turn. Brognola packed his videotape and maps into his attaché case, joined the others around the conference table.

"We'll be landing at Miami in one minute. You gentlemen will be in Peru sometime tonight. One thing I want to stress: this is a soft probe. We need information. Not a body count."

The three warriors of Mack Bolan's Able Team glanced at the weapons and ammunition covering the tables, the full-auto shotgun, the assault rifles, the silenced Beretta pistols. Lyons and Gadgets and Blancanales looked to one another, exchanged shakes of the head.

"Sure, Hal," said Lyons, smiling. "Anything you say."

3

Dawn light on the snow of the Andes flashed like sheets of pale flame. Outside the small ports of the DC-3, peaks and sheer cliff faces rose against the heavens, which were still night-violet and shot with stars. Gadgets pressed an Instamatic camera against the glass and snapped a photo.

"Tourist," Lyons joked above the roar and rattle of the old plane.

"Damn right! Federal fringe benefit." Gadgets tucked the camera into a pocket of his pack, then returned to assembling his gear.

With their breath clouding about them in the freezing cargo area, Able Team had packed and repacked the field gear. Because they would have local people guiding them to the hidden reactor complex, the three Americans had packed few rations. They carried only high-protein wafers and vitamin supplements; they would have to depend on the Indians contracted by the CIA to provide their meals.

But they would not travel light. Lyons struggled to arrange his weapons' magazines on his bandoliers. Some of the heavy box mags for the assault shotgun went on his chest bandolier, the other mags in the side pockets of his pack. He stripped a couple of the magazine pouches holding 9mm subsonic cartridges for his Beretta from the web belt, stashed those in other pack pockets. He attached a pouch to the web belt to carry speedloaders for the Magnum. Then he twisted his torso, flexed his chest to test the positioning of his shoulder-holstered Python. The Python's grip tapped against a magazine. It took minutes for him to slightly shift the position of the shoulder holster.

Blancanales glanced up from his packing and watched Lyons shoulder his pack and shotgun, then stand. Lyons lurched a few steps.

"I know why they call you 'Ironman,'" Blancanales shouted.

"What?" Lyons shouted back.

Blancanales pointed to the .357 Magnum revolver and Beretta auto-pistol that Lyons wore, and the assault shotgun that he held. "Because you carry so much iron."

Squatting down beside his friend, Lyons shouted, "Long life through superior fire power."

Laughing, Blancanales went back to his gear. For Able Team, life itself was a permanent condition of prebattle nerves. Blancanales too had many pounds of ammunition to carry, and it was a relief of tension to laugh about it. He had three hundred rounds of 5.56mm ammo in ten magazines to cope with, plus the heavy 40mm grenades. Konzaki had packed a box of assorted grenades: buckshot, high-explosive and phosphorous. As each grenade weighed a pound, Blancanales decided to take only thirteen, a buckshot round to carry in the M-16/M-203 as they moved, eleven high-explosive and phosphorous rounds, and an extra round of buckshot. Surveying the quantity of ammunition he would carry, he muttered, "Soft probe...bullshit."

As the electronics specialist, Gadgets packed only five magazines of 5.56mm cartridges for his small CAR-15. But he carried the heavy shortwave transmitter and all the accessories—the scrambler and screech unit to encode and decode their communications and the long antenna of metal tape to insure the radio link with Stony Man. He also carried two miniature microphones and a receiver. He sealed all the electronic units in 10-mil vinyl bags, then padded the radio and coding units with his other gear—the disposable plastic anticontamination suit, his poncho, protein rations, the aluminum and foam case for the micro-transmitters. The clutter of gear added a measure of protection.

Shouldering his pack and standing, Gadgets groaned. "Oh, man! Am I the mule."

"What's your problem?" Lyons shouted.

"This shortwave set. Next time, we go where they have telephones!"

The pilots' compartment door opened. Horizontal through the plane's windshields, the light of the rising sun filled the cargo area. The copilot walked back to them. He wore a fur-collared Eisenhower jacket and tight Levi's. Able Team did not know his name. When they had changed planes at an airfield somewhere back in the Peruvian mountains, the pilots had stayed in the cockpit. He did not introduce himself now.

He went to one knee near their gear and gazed at the weapons. Then he observed their lightweight clothing— Gadgets and Blancanales in green camouflage fatigues, Lyons in faded shadow-gray cotton fatigues.

"Cold enough for you?"

"Didn't notice," Blancanales shouted back. "Been busy."

"You all know where you're going? Who you're meeting?"

"We thought you knew!" Lyons answered, slapping his forehead in mock surprise. "Now we're all screwed up."

The copilot laughed sarcastically. "A joker. Dig this

dude. Whoever sent you doesn't like you. 'Cause you're going to a place called the Stone Age. Where the snake is king. Where Satan ain't born yet—and when he is, he's going to hightail it out.''

His eyes wide with shock and amazement, Lyons looked to Gadgets and Blancanales, then back to the co-pilot. "But the travel agent said it would be nice...so unspoiled...like Hawaii, but without the crowds."

Still sneering, the copilot shook his head. "Hope you keep your sense of humor down there. Now listen," he said, warming to these cavalier characters, "you're in luck. You'll have a good man waiting for you at the air-strip. He'll hold your hand, try to keep you alive. When my plane went down, he's the man who found me and brought me out. Just you all treat him like the proud son of a bitch he is, and you'll get along fine."

The plane lost altitude. They felt the atmospheric pressure pushing at their ears. The copilot gave a quick salute and started back to the cockpit.

Lyons called out, "Hey! Tell us what goes on!"

Laughing, the copilot shook his head no. "And spoil the surprises? *If* you come back, we'll swap stories." Still grinning, he closed the cockpit door behind him.

"Well, what do you make of that?" Lyons asked the others.

"He's the joker," Gadgets smiled. He went to a port and looked out. He hurried back to his pack and re-trieved the Instamatic. "Take a look out there. Beauti-ful!"

Blancanales whistled as he peered out. "A world of green."

They saw no highways, no farmlands, no towns. Be-hind them, the Andes had become forested foothills. Swirls of clouds fanned out over green flatlands. Here and there, rainstorms swept over the jungle. Other regions glowed with the amber light of the searing tropical morning. The plane passed over a river, the water black, flashing with sunlight. Then they saw their first sign of civilization.

"Someone's got a motorboat down there," Lyons pointed. "Maybe they're waterskiing."

Blancanales focused his binoculars on the river. "That's no boat. That's a barge."

"Barge? It's too small."

"Check it out." He handed Lyons the binoculars. "It looks small because the river's about a half mile wide."

"Wow...you're right." Panning away from the sliver of water beneath them, Lyons scanned the vast carpet of unbroken jungle extending to the far horizon. "Oh, man, oh, man. Does that add perspective to what I'm looking at."

"Wherever we're going, whatever we're doing," Gadgets said as he snapped a panorama of three photos, "I sure hope we don't have to walk home."

Seconds after the DC-3 touched down, the copilot threw open the cockpit door and paced urgently down the length of the swaying plane as it taxied. He had shed his heavy coat, now wore a bright purple T-shirt tucked into his jeans. He grabbed the handstrap at the door to steady himself as he worked the latch lever. He pushed the door open.

"Move it, passengers! In three minutes, this here aircraft is back in the sky."

The copilot jerked a rope-handled crate to the doorway, waited until the plane slowed to a stop. Then he jumped out and pulled the crate after him.

Able Team followed him, one man after another, dropping the four feet to a field of mud. The hot, wet air closed around them like steam. In seconds, sweat beaded their faces.

The airstrip paralleled a river. Bulldozers had scraped

a long straight flat on the riverbank. Huge piles of tangled brush and branches rotted in the mud at each end of the strip. An improvised dock of fifty-five-gallon drums extended a hundred feet into the slow, silt-dark river; rough-sawn planks lashed to the drums served as a walkway.

The copilot dragged the crate across the field. Six black men waited for him. The men were nearly naked, wearing only loincloths and weapons. Some held old shotguns, one man an M-1 carbine, one man a bow and long arrows.

"Black Indians?" Blancanales wondered out loud.

They slogged through the mud. As the three uniformed and well-equipped soldiers from the United States neared the group, they studied the Indians. The Indians ignored them. They gathered around the copilot as he clawed at the lid of the crate.

The Indians were not Negroes. Black paint covered the mahogany-brown skin. Some wore the paint solid. Some wore the paint in patterns. One man had his body and face black except for a rectangle around his eyes. Another wore the paint in horizontal bands across his body, like a snake's markings.

All the Indians wore their hair in knife-cut black bowls on top of their heads, their temples and necks shaved bare. They had either bones or feathers through their earlobes. At their waists, thongs of leather secured their loincloths. Web belts carried ammunition pouches and sheath knives. Most of the men wore leather sandals. One man sported rotting orange-and-blue jogging shoes.

Laughter and chatter broke out as the copilot lifted away the crate top. Inside, there were pump-action shotguns, machetes, boxes of cartridges, and plastic-wrapped packages. The copilot passed the first shotgun to the Indian who carried the M-1 carbine.

Stroking the Parkerized finish, the Indian turned the Remington 870 twenty-inch shotgun over in his hands. He touched the black plastic of the stock and foregrip, pumped the action, snapped the trigger at the sky. He took a shotgun cartridge from a belt pouch, held it up against the extended magazine. He counted space for six cartridges. He grinned a white, perfect smile and slapped the copilot on the back. The copilot passed out shotguns to the other five Indians.

Overwhelmed by their good fortune, the group laughed and clacked actions and snapped triggers. The copilot and the apparent Indian leader—the man with the rectangle around his eyes—stepped away from the others. They talked in English for a few seconds, the Indian shaking the copilot's hand. Then the Indian's eyes fixed on the purple of the copilot's T-shirt for a moment. In an instant, the copilot pulled off the T-shirt and gave it to the Indian.

Blancanales nudged Lyons and Gadgets and told them, "That was a routine. The pilot didn't have that shirt on until we landed. He put it on so that he could give it away."

The copilot gestured toward the three waiting North Americans. The Indian looked at them and smiled his white flash. He waved as the copilot sprinted bare chested to the DC-3 and pulled himself up through the door. In thirty seconds, the plane was roaring over the distant treetops.

Only after the sound of the DC-3's engines had faded to nothing did the Indian turn to Able Team. Slinging his new shotgun over his shoulder, he came close to them. He extended his hand and spoke in curiously soft English. "Hello. Pleased to meet you. I am Thomas Jefferson Xavante. And I will take you to the city of slavery and death."

4

Following two Indian point men along a pathway through the stinking yet sometimes fragrant half darkness of the jungle, Lyons heard Blancanales and the Indian named Thomas Jefferson talking in English and Spanish and Portuguese. After introducing himself at the airfield, the Indian leader had said there was no time for questions, that they must move quickly, before the army came.

The Indians had loaded and slung their new Remington shotguns, then hacked apart the wooden shipping crate with their new black-bladed machetes and burned the wood. Each man had also received black nylon bandoliers and two boxes of shotgun shells. Now, they carried both their old weapons and their new Remingtons, the cartridge boxes and the plastic-wrapped bundles. The line of Indians wove quickly through a maze of trails, shoving fronds and branches and giant elephant-ear leaves aside with their shoulders.

The line of men moved through the shadowy darkness of triple-canopy rain forest. Above them, the tops of hundred-foot-tall trees shadowed a second layer of smaller trees. Below the lowest branches of the two levels of tree foliage, the ferns and vines and flowering plants blocked the last specks of direct sunlight.

As the men left the river miles behind, the heat became total. No leaf or frond moved unless they touched it, no wind stirred the heavy, dank air. Lyons sweated like never before in his life. Sweat completely soaked his faded gray fatigues before he had walked the first mile. Soon, sweat ran from the cuffs of his shirt. He felt sweat flowing down his legs. Sweat trickling from his close-cut hair stung his eyes.

Insects found his sweat. Flies wandered on his face until he wiped them away. Small beetles clung like multicolored buttons on his gray uniform. He heard a droning. He searched for the insect making the sound, looking above him, behind him. Finally he saw it: a wasp the size of a small bird. He flinched away, horrified, blundered into a fern silky with spiderwebs. An orange-and-violet-and-red spider tried to capture him. Lyons thrashed free. The Indian point men glanced back, laughed.

In the distance, they heard a cacophony of bird songs and screeches. But when the men neared, despite their stealth, the birds went quiet. Only the insect sounds continued.

After an hour or more of walking, one of the point men came back to Lyons and motioned for him to pause. The Indian squatted. Lyons looked up the trail, couldn't see the first man. Lyons squatted, his knees almost touching the Indian, waited. Lyons took a squeeze bottle of insect repellent out of his thigh pocket and smeared it on his face and neck.

The Indian watched, his eyes white half coins in the black of his painted face. Lyons saw the Indian's eyes follow the bottle. Lyons held up the bottle, motioned for the Indian to watch. Then Lyons smeared the repellent on his left hand and wrist. Putting down the bottle, Lyons held up his hands to the flies and tiny beetles buzzing around him. Mimicking him, the Indian held up his hands.

Flies attacked both of Lyons's hands. An iridescent black fly with gray thousand-faceted eyes landed on the back of his left hand and immediately put a sucker through the skin. Lyons slapped it away. The fly came at his face. He grabbed it out of the air, slammed it into the leaves and mud of the trail, hit it twice with his fist before it stopped moving.

Grinning, the Indian still held up his hands. No insects landed on his blackened skin. Puzzled, Lyons rubbed the back of his right hand over the Indian's arm. A smear of black came away. Lyons watched as insects alighted on his white skin but avoided his blackened skin. The Indian nodded. Then his eyes whipped up the trail.

For a second, Lyons heard nothing. A young boy walked toward them. The boy was naked except for black body paint and a necklace of brilliant blue feathers. He called out to the men. When he saw Lyons, he stared, then ran back. The Indians laughed, followed the boy.

Smoke from a fire swirled in a small clearing. Above a circle of ferns and trampled grass twenty yards across, the trees closed, creating a dome of interlaced branches. Flowering vines splashed the green walls with lurid colors.

A cool breeze carrying the odors of river water and burning wood touched Lyons's face. The point man sat at the fire, poked at something. Lyons and the other men joined him.

"We eat," Thomas Jefferson Xavante told him. "Then we take boats to the next camp."

"How's it going, Ironman?" Blancanales sat beside Lyons. "Looks like you went swimming."

"Yeah." Lyons slipped out of his shoulder holster and bandoliers, took off his long-sleeved shirt. He wrung it out. He draped it over his backpack and Atchisson assault shotgun to dry.

Gadgets sat down and leaned back on his pack as if it was an easy chair. "What's for breakfast?"

Blancanales glanced into the fire's ashes and stones. "Looks like turtle."

"Hmm, a delicacy." Gadgets pulled a Swiss Army knife from one of his pockets and folded out a fork from it.

"So what did you find out from the men?" Lyons asked Blancanales. "Where's that city he talked about? Is it the place we're looking for?"

"We look at your maps, we talk," Thomas told Lyons, taking a seat beside him. The boy sat with him. "This is my son, Abraham Lincoln Xavante. What are your names, sir?"

Lyons hesitated, glanced at Blancanales and Gadgets, then answered, "Ironman."

"And I'm the Politician."

"You can call me Gadgets."

Thomas frowned, offended. Then he flashed his brilliant smile again. "I forget. You are secret agents. You can no give me names. No can? Do not?" He struggled to find the correct words.

"Can't," Blancanales advised. "Your English is excellent, Thomas Jefferson. You speak Spanish and Portuguese also, right?"

"Yes. And my people's language. And languages of other peoples, other tribes. I study in mission school, many years. Then read books, hear radio, see television. I study history of America. I take name of your President Jefferson, give my son name of President Lincoln, give other son name Simón Bolívar."

"What denomination was the mission?" Lyons asked. When he saw Thomas did not understand the word, he said, "What church? Catholic? Protestant? Mormon?"

"This is my church." Thomas gestured to the living cathedral over them. "No need Jehovah, Jesus, Mary. I only want your Constitution. Now we look at maps. Abraham! Bring food." Thomas spoke a few quick words in his own language. The boy hurried away.

Blancanales unfolded a plastic-coated map and located the position of the river airstrip. Thomas leaned across Lyons and traced a line with his finger from the river to a tributary.

"We take boats now. Two hours, three hours we back on same river."

"Then why did we walk overland?" Lyons asked.

Thomas pointed to the map again, to a bend in the river. "Mission school there. Army sometimes come. Priests see us, they tell army."

Abraham returned with a folded leaf the size of a shopping bag. The other Indians gathered around, smiling, watching the foreigners.

"The appetizers!" Thomas exclaimed. "We eat!"

A tangled mass of caterpillars squirmed on the leaf. Barely suppressing a laugh, Thomas took one, popped it into his mouth. He watched the three North Americans as he took several more, threw the handful in his mouth. The tail of one whipped about on his lips until he sucked it in.

His stomach heaving, Lyons watched Blancanales take a caterpillar and eat it. Blancanales took another one, bit off the head, looked at the oozing fluids, then finished it. Gadgets saw Lyons not eating.

"Hey, man. Get with it. High protein."

"Think of them as sushi," Blancanales told him. "You're at a Japanese restaurant eating raw fish. Sea anemones. Except they're still moving. Once you get past that, the taste is all right."

Lyons stared at the caterpillars. They writhed their fat bodies against the slick leaf. Some were blue and white, some bright yellow, others reddish. Some of them had long waving antennae.

Blancanales leaned toward Lyons and told him, "You have to. It's one of the rules of indigenous operations.

Eat their food, talk their language, sleep with their girls. Go to it.''

Reaching out, Lyons glanced up, saw all the Indians watching him. He steeled his gut, took one of the wriggling larvae. It was warm in his fingers. Keeping his eyes on the Indians, he thought of egg rolls in a Chinese restaurant and tossed the caterpillar into his mouth. It knotted itself up on his tongue in the long instant before his jaws closed.

Like a half-melted chocolate, it squashed between his teeth. Only after he swallowed did he taste it. A flavor not unlike chicken cream soup. He liked it. He grabbed three more, gulped them. Again, the cream-soup flavor, but with accents of spices he couldn't identify.

''Hey, they're great!'' he told Thomas.

All the Indians laughed. Thomas slapped him on the back, shook his hand. Then Thomas reached into the fire's embers, pulled out a blackened tin can.

''Now try some grasshoppers!''

After their meal of caterpillars, roast cicadas, and baked-in-the-shell turtle, Thomas told Able Team what he knew of their mission's objective. ''Two years ago, the army comes. They have machines, boats, helicopters. The soldiers take many Indians, make them slaves. If Indians no work, army shoot. Soldiers make camp for slaves. Sharp wire, high houses with machine guns. Many dogs. But Indians live. Sometimes we attack when they cut jungle. We kill soldiers. Save some Indians. So army get fast boats, boats that fly. More fences. Bombs. Man step on bomb, legs gone.

''First, they make road, then dig great holes. Holes bigger than trucks, bigger than many trucks. River boats bring much concrete, long steel. They make concrete buildings in holes. Much of building in hole, only top of building above dirt.

"More Europeans and Chinese come, with many machines—"

"Europeans? Chinese?" Blancanales interrupted.

"Yes. Many. Maybe North Americans. They have light hair, light skin. Chinese never work, only watch. Sometimes kill Indians. Maybe the Chinese the boss. They bring new machines, make electricity. Make place like *Dr. No*, in movie. You see James Bond? Like that...."

"Were you in there?" Lyons asked.

"No. Later some Indians escape. Boats come from mountains, bring yellow sand. The army, the Europeans, the Chinese, they never touch sand. Only Indians. Soldiers wear mask. Soldiers who drive trucks wear mask.

"There is fire. Much fire, not water. Sometimes smoke that kills, one minute and—dead. Soldiers wear suits like spacemen. Indians work, then much sickness. Many Indians sick. Hair fall off, skin fall off, teeth fall off.

"Soldiers take Indians to river, machine-gun. But not all die. We help, they live month, two month. Then they die. Strange things on hands, feet. Sometimes in body— here." Thomas thumped his chest.

"Did you take them to doctors?" Blancanales asked.

"Doctors?" Thomas almost spat the word. "Government doctors? Army doctors? We take sick men to church station, one night helicopter comes. Many soldiers."

"Are you sure it was the army? Brazilian army?" Lyons pressed.

"I know army. In time of my father, grandfather, army takes Indians. They are slaves on railroad, on boats. Then for many years, no more slavery. Some government people help Indians, some soldiers build roads with machines. But then army comes to build the city, they take Indians for slaves. Same as old times.''

"Where is their territory?'' Lyons asked. ''Do they have patrols?''

"Soldiers guard city. Leave only to take slaves. Find villages, attack. Take men, take women.''

Blancanales studied the map and pointed to their position. "We are in Bolivia now. Do the soldiers attack Bolivian Indians?''

"Map means nothing. Never see soldiers of Bolivia. They camp on roads, stay in trucks. No government here.''

"Let's go, gentlemen.'' Lyons gathered up his equipment. "Enough talk. Time to make distance.''

Thomas issued instructions to his men. His son scattered the ashes of the fire with a stick. As the smoke dissipated, the insects returned. Flies found Lyons's bare skin. He swatted at them with his wet shirt, then slipped on the shirt and pulled the collar up to protect his neck.

Across the clearing, he saw one of the Indians touching up his black body paint. Lyons went to him and squatted down to watch. The Indian squeezed the juice of a fruit into a can, then added pinches of a powdered herb and stirred. He smeared the black mixture onto his skin.

The Indian offered the can to Lyons. Lyons smelled the juice. It had an odd greasy-bitter smell. The Indian stuck a finger in the can and drew a stripe across Lyons's face.

Lyons held the can up to the flies. None of them came near the can. Stripping off his shirt, he smeared the juice on his shoulders and neck. Insects landed on his arms, and he smeared the last of the mixture there.

Gathering up weapons and cartridge boxes, the Indian pointed to an uncrushed fruit and said, "Genipap."

"Ge-ni-pap," Lyons repeated.

Thomas and Blancanales left the clearing. Gadgets shouldered his backpack and followed. Lyons kept the can and fruit, returned to his equipment. He slipped on his shoulder holster and bandoliers, draped his wet shirt over his pack, jogged after the others.

Insects bit his unprotected skin. The fruit and soot-blackened can in one hand, the Atchisson in the other, he couldn't swat the flies away. He twisted and jerked as he walked, the flies lifting away for an instant, then returning.

He didn't suffer long. In a few minutes, they came to a stagnant stream overhung with branches. Fragments of midday light flashed on the green water. Lyons squinted against the sudden brilliance, saw on the muddy slopes several canoes camouflaged with brush.

Indians threw aside the branches and fronds. They stacked their boxes and packages in the fire-hollowed interiors of the boats. Blancanales and Gadgets passed them their packs. While the others arranged the equipment, Lyons squatted at the water's edge and squeezed genipap juice into the battered can. He dipped the can in the scummy water to thin the juice, then dabbed the mixture on his torso. Blancanales watched him.

"Go easy on that stuff," he told Lyons. "There's no way to know what it is."

"I don't care what it is, the bugs don't like it. It's definitely going to save my white skin."

Thomas saw Lyons blacking his body. "Good. On skin. Face. Hair. Make you not look like *civilizado*."

Lyons squeezed the last of the juice out of the fruit and massaged it into his hair and sideburns.

Jaws a foot wide snapped at him. Rising from the

stagnant shallow, a ten-foot-long crocodile opened its jaws to take Lyons's legs. Scrambling backward, digging in his heels and feeling his boots slide in the ooze, Lyons looked into the mouth of the reptile. The jaws opened impossibly wide, exposing jagged rows of teeth. Lyons clawed at the bank, his fingers slipping in the slime.

The jaws ripped away a strip of his pant leg. Lyons heard himself crying out as the crocodile gained another few inches. As the jaws yawned again, Lyons tore his Python from his shoulder holster. He stuck his arm out, the muzzle of the revolver only inches from the pink flesh of the creature's upper palate.

The 158-grain jacketed hollowpoint slug punched through the soft tissues and exploded from the top of the reptile's skull, the impact snapping the crocodile's head back and killing it instantly. Brain gone, its head flopped forward and lay still in the mud. The unblinking eyes bulged from the sockets.

Even as nerve spasms twitched the tail, the Indians crowded past Lyons and dragged the reptile up from the water. They pulled it to higher ground and set about butchering it with their machetes.

Lyons sat on the water's edge, his Colt Python still in his hand. He stared at his ripped pant leg.

"Good, good, Ironman," Thomas congratulated him. "Much meat, meat for everyone."

Gadgets called out to him. "That insect repellent attracts crocodiles. I'd rather get bitten by a fly anytime!"

5

All through the afternoon, Blancanales floated in a green world. The Indians—one man at each end of the narrow canoe—paddled without pause for hours, leaning deep into each stroke, alternating their strokes from side to side. Blancanales sat low in the boat, reclining against his pack, only his knees and face showing above the sides. He had offered to help row, but the Indians pointed to the jungle, touched their eyes, pointed at Blancanales. Blancanales nodded his understanding, radioed Lyons and Gadgets to stay low and unseen.

They passed riverbanks tangled with roots, shallows choked with fallen trees, mud slopes crowded with crocodiles. River birds startled from the water in sheets of winged color. They passed unending walls of jungle. Often, the outspread branches of the huge trees closed over the narrow river, creating a hundred-foot-high tunnel.

Abraham rode in Lyons's boat. He played bamboo panpipes from time to time, the fluting melodies drifting over the water to Blancanales, who also heard the boy's laughter as Lyons tried the panpipes.

Lyons buzzed Blancanales on his hand radio. "Hey, Politician. You know what? This kid knows the Gettysburg Address by memory. Word for word."

Shadow claimed the river as the sun fell in the sky. Blancanales pushed back the camouflage-patterned crush hat he wore, looked up at the sky, checked his watch. Sundown would come in two hours. He keyed his hand radio and said to Gadgets, "Mr. Wizard, ask Thomas Jefferson when we'll make camp. We're losing daylight."

After a pause, Thomas's voice answered. "Soon. Maybe hour. Then we stay at village. I like this radio. Maybe we get radios. Is possible?"

"We can work out a deal."

A whistle came from the shore. The Indian boatmen stopped their rowing. The whistle rose and fell. Blancanales's radio buzzed: "This is Thomas. We go to shore now. Please, I speak with men...."

Blancanales and Lyons held up their hand radios. The boatmen had heard radios before, but never the broadcast of words in their own language. They recognized Thomas's voice, listened to his instructions. They kept looking across the water to Thomas, then looking at the radio. After his voice cut off, Blancanales and Lyons acknowledged.

"Got the message here," Lyons told him.

"These men heard it, too."

The boatmen saw the foreigners speaking, then tried to speak, also, all four chattering and shouting into the microphones. Thomas had to shout at them across the water to stop the noise. After checking their shotguns and putting the weapons at their feet, they paddled for the riverbank.

Blancanales did not see the waiting warriors until the boats touched the weeds and knotted roots of the shore. Black with body paint, the men left cover and helped pull the dugout canoes onto the bank. They carried bows and arrows, spears, old single-shot shotguns. There were no greetings, no friendly chatter. Some of the men and boys stared at the North Americans, but the others spoke quickly with Thomas, gestured to the north with their weapons.

Thomas turned to Able Team. "I am not chief. Molomano is chief. Fight soldiers many times, lose men. Much sadness with women. Children hungry. When soldiers near, Molomano no fight. Always run. But soldiers find village this day, attack. Take some men for slaves. All other people run away, hide here. This good chance for you to make many friends, make Molomano strong chief again. I tell him three *civilizados* come from United States to help fight soldiers. That good story, yes? We fight soldiers?"

"We want prisoners. Soldiers to question."

"Question, then kill, yes?"

Groups of Indians clustered along the trail. Voices greeted Thomas and his men. But when the tribespeople saw the foreigners, they went quiet. Children ran behind their mothers, young boys gripped their stick spears. Nursing mothers covered their babies.

In a glance, Blancanales spotted malnutrition and vitamin deficiencies in many of the people. Like the warriors with Thomas, the men wore loincloths. Children wore nothing. Most of the women were dressed in shapeless handwoven robes belted with braided fibers. One pregnant teenager wore a faded red football jersey, her seven-month belly stretching the number 10. Many of the people had running sores, spindly arms and legs. The babies of women with shriveled breasts cried continuously, always hungry for milk their mothers didn't have. Older children had the distended bellies of malnutrition.

Thomas strode through the gathered tribe, calling out to the people, pointing from Lyons to the loads of crocodile meat his men carried. Flies and insects covered the meat, buzzed in swirls as Thomas pantomimed Lyons shooting the reptile. The people turned to Lyons, stared at the shirtless white man with the blackened body and face.

Blancanales leaned to Lyons, spoke in a low voice. "Notice that he left out the screaming and crawling."

"Hey! You look down the throat of a crocodile and keep your cool."

"Pol!" Gadgets hissed. "Catch his act. You could learn something."

They watched as Thomas described in words and sounds and pantomime the DC-3 coming out of the sky. He slipped the Remington 870 from his shoulder, presented it to Molomano.

Puzzled by the unfamiliar weapon, the chief pointed it at the sky, pulled the trigger. It was unloaded. He looked for the latch to hinge the shotgun open as if it were a single-shot. Thomas pointed to the foregrip, moved his hand in a pump motion.

Jerking back the pump, slamming it forward, the chief chambered a round and aimed at a tree. The weapon didn't fire. Thomas reached out, pushed the safety across. The chief aimed again, fired.

Leaves and twigs showered the trail. Chief Molomano grinned. Thomas made the pumping motion again and again. Chambering shell after shell, the chief fired five more times.

Jumping with excitement, Molomano flourished the shotgun in the air, shouted to his warriors. They shouted, waved their spears and old shotguns.

Thomas called out to Able Team, "Shoot your guns!"

Gadgets and Blancanales fired three bursts from their auto-rifles; Lyons pulled out his Python, fired an instant later. The pistol's deafening blast brought laughter from the tribesmen. Thomas held up his M-1 carbine, pointed to the north. All the men shouted, waved their weapons.

Thomas went to Able Team. "It is agreed," he told

them, slinging his M-1 over his shoulder. "Tonight, we kill soldiers."

An hour before dark they were heading west. Three tribesmen—Molomano and two warriors—accompanied Able Team and Thomas's fighters. They carried only weapons and ammunition. For the first mile, the line moved at a steady, jogging pace. Point men sprinted far ahead to scout parallel trails and check possible ambush sites before dark.

Lyons realized Able Team slowed the Indians. The black-painted men ran effortlessly and unconsciously, their sweat-glistening legs flashing in the fading light. From time to time, they forgot the North Americans, leaving the three men behind. Then they glanced back, slacked their strides until the clothed and weapons-heavy Able Team closed the line.

Counting in pounds, Lyons totalled the weight of the weapons and ammunition he carried. The Atchisson, almost ten pounds loaded. Four extra magazines of 12-gauge, five pounds. The Beretta and two twenty-round magazines, four pounds. And then the weight of his Python.

Behind him, Blancanales and Gadgets carried almost as much weight. With every step, their boots shattered the silence of the ferns and hardwoods. The Indians' feet skipped over the bedding of dead leaves and wood and living vines without a sound, the tribesmen barefooted, Thomas and his men in water-softened leather sandals.

Miles later, as night closed on them, they reached the point men. The paths had taken the twelve men from one side to the other of a fold in the river. Thomas, Molomano and the point men huddled in a whispered exchange for a minute. Thomas then took the information to the three foreigners. "Soldiers camp in the village. They have boats. Big boats with lights, machine guns. Big for many men. Two boats that fly. . . ."

"What do you mean, 'that fly'?" Lyons asked.

"I do not know the word. They have propeller in back end, two men, maybe three ride. It not touch water."

"Air cushion!" Gadgets told them. He asked Thomas: "They spray water out the sides?"

"Yes, yes. And some shoot machine gun. Some bombs. Fly over water, over sand—"

"And the soldiers?" Lyons interrupted.

"Many. Some on boat, some in village. They have many Indian people for slaves. Some of this tribe, some of other tribe."

"And did your men see the guard around the camp? What are their positions?" Blancanales asked.

"Many. They saw soldiers putting bombs around village. Bombs with long string, if touch string, boom. Like a hundred shotguns. Other bombs with electric wire. If soldiers see Indian, hear Indian, turn on bomb."

"Claymore," Gadgets concluded.

"No fun," Lyons said. "Going up against claymores in the dark, in the jungle."

"Who says we have to slip in on land?" Gadgets asked.

"Get boats, float down on the current," Blancanales nodded.

Gadgets completed the plan. "Take their transportation away, we can come back for the soldiers in the daylight. Or ambush them if they try to escape overland."

Thomas shook his head. "Boats in village."

"Could we swim?" Blancanales asked.

"Crocodiles!" Lyons answered.

"We call caimans." Thomas told them. "And piranha. Snakes. Very dangerous. Sometimes caimans attack, like Ironman."

"I'd like to avoid the river," Lyons stressed.

"Hey, man," Gadgets joked. "Me and the Politician could do it. We're not wearing any of that lizard- attracting lotion."

Blancanales and Gadgets laughed softly. Lyons didn't think it was funny.

"All right," Blancanales said finally. "Looks like we crawl. Thomas, you and me go in first. Then we'll lead Gadgets and Ironman in...."

"We'll use the Berettas," Lyons continued the planning. "Maybe we can do it ourselves. But if shooting starts...."

"Only us?" Thomas asked, incredulous.

"Molomano and all the others can circle the camp and give us backup if we need it," Lyons added.

"Against many soldiers?" Thomas questioned. "How can only four men attack many soldiers?"

Gadgets slipped out his Beretta 93-R and held it up against the last gray light of day. "With silence."

6

Snaking through the darkness, Blancanales felt for trip lines with a length of dry river grass. The point men had said the soldiers set the claymores and trip lines at waist height, but Blancanales took no chances. He stayed low, crawling on his belly, sometimes turning over and waving the blade of grass above him. After each advance of a few feet, Thomas crawled up.

No clanking weapon or snagged bandolier would betray the men. Neither man carried a shotgun or rifle. Blancanales wore no web belt or holster; the Beretta rode in a thigh pocket, his radio in the other pocket, his knife in his boot. Thomas carried only a black-bladed machete.

Thirty yards from the camp, a fallen tree four feet in diameter blocked their approach. Blancanales did not want to risk hopping over. He felt along the trunk until he came to a gap. He moved infinitely slowly, carefully. This was a perfect position for a sentry or a booby trap. For a minute, he lay still, listening. He flicked a bit of wood into the ferns, listening for the click of a rifle safety or the noises of a soldier shifting his weight. He heard nothing.

He waved the blade of river grass across the gap, from the earth up. At knee height, it snagged. He pushed the dry grass against the snag, slid the grass from side to side. He reached out with his left hand, felt the slick monofilament.

"Hsst! Thomas!" Blancanales called him forward. The Indian moved silently. When Thomas touched him, Blancanales whispered, "Bomb here. Wait. Don't move."

Blancanales slithered under the trip line. Touching the monofilament with the grass blade, he followed it to the left. He found it knotted around a branch. He went to the other end. He found the claymore by the slightest touch, waved the blade of grass everywhere around it. A smart soldier would have put a second booby trap on the first to kill an intruder attempting to defuse the claymore. In fact, Blancanales thought, a smart soldier would have placed the claymore so that it killed not only the first man through the gap in the fallen tree, but any other men behind him.

In the darkness, he touched the outlines of the antipersonnel weapon, his fingers tracing the outlines of a thin rectangular block. He felt the convex face, the concave back. He touched the raised letters on the face, reading the words by memory: FRONT TOWARD ENEMY.

An M18A1 Anti-Personnel Mine. U.S. Army equipment. Blancanales found the fuse with his fingers. More American equipment—an M-1 Pull-Firing Device.

This is a trip down memory lane, Blancanales thought as he worked. The soldier who placed this claymore wouldn't have made it out of Fort Benning. He would have had his ass kicked up to his shirt collar. Leaving the safety pin hanging. Makes it just too easy.

Blancanales slipped the cotter pin through the striker housing, then cut the rope lashing the claymore to a branch. He took the claymore and wound up the monofilament, then placed the claymore in the gap in the fallen tree where he could find it later. He and Thomas continued forward.

Close now to the river and the soldiers, Blancanales

and Thomas heard voices. They smelled burning wood and meat. Fragments of light broke through the trees and ferns screening them from the camp, smoke swirling in the light. Shafts of light flickered above them as they searched for the next booby trap.

They cut east, toward the riverbank. In the next hour, they zigzagged through the darkness and found and defused three more claymores.

Finally, Blancanales keyed his hand radio, whispered, ''No real problems so far. Completed half circle. Will now check out village.''

Leaving the jungle behind, they crawled through tree stumps and low brush. The burned village still smoldered, cloaking the area in smoke. Blancanales and Thomas no longer had to find their way by touch. The smoke above them glowed with the lights from the boat and from the soldiers' camp.

To their right, they saw the river. A fifty-foot patrol craft floated a few feet from shore, a gangplank extending from the boat's side to the sand. The craft also served as a troop shuttle. Behind the cabin and bridge, a canvas awning roofed a deck. Blancanales spotted a soldier manning a forward machine gun. The soldier sat on the small deck in front of the cabin, his back to the village. He stared out at the shimmering water, smoked, raised a bottle to drink. No one manned the machine gun at the rear of the craft.

Two air-cushion boats were parked on the sand. Two soldiers sat on the snub bow of one boat, smoking and talking in loud voices. That boat carried a machine gun. The other boat, a few steps away, carried a blunt-muzzled heavy weapon that Blancanales did not recognize.

Again, the two silent, patient warriors slithered in zigzags, searching for claymores. They found two more trip lines, dismantled the booby traps. With the aid of the diffuse illumination, Blancanales gave Thomas a lesson in defusing the antipersonnel devices, silently demonstrating each detail in the deadly and meticulous work. When they finished with each claymore, they set it aside to be retrieved later.

Finally, they completed the second semicircle around the camp. They had swept the booby traps from the south end of the village. Lying still for minutes, they listened to the activity inside the camp. Piles of ash and smoking debris separated them from the soldiers.

Silhouetted against the lights, they saw rows of heads, shoulder to shoulder. The forms shifted and turned, but never stood. Soldiers with auto-rifles in their hands paced in front of the seated people. A baby wailed.

"Indians," Thomas whispered. "Will be slaves."

Soldiers walked to one of the forms, jerked a man to his feet. The man was not an Indian. He wore olive drab, the fatigue pants tucked into the tops of his boots. As the prisoner passed a light, Blancanales saw the man's light skin, his mustache, his hands tied behind his back. His uniform shirt had unit patches on the sleeves.

"Army of Brazil!" Thomas whispered quickly.

"Interesting..." Blancanales said, keying his hand radio. "We're twenty-five, thirty feet from them," he reported. "I count thirteen captives. One of them is a Brazilian army officer."

"No doubt about it?" Lyons asked.

"He's got the uniform on. Stand by, we're coming out."

They continued the crawl, double-checking for booby traps. They left the lights and noise of the soldiers behind them and entered the darkness of the trees. The two men inched along a worn footpath, Blancanales waving the dry spine of a fern frond ahead of him. He found one more trip line and defused the claymore by touch.

A half hour passed before they rejoined the others. Blancanales gave his report in a whisper. "We cleared this trail straight into the village. You got intermittent jungle and logs, then a cut-and-cleared area around the village. The huts are burned down. Clean lines of fire from the edge of the village to the soldiers."

"How many soldiers?" Lyons asked.

"I counted eight in the open. But there must be more, maybe sleeping, maybe in the patrol boat."

"So you got a plan, man?" Gadgets jived.

"Just like we talked. We three first. Thomas and all the other men deploy on the south side."

Lyons turned to Thomas. "Tell your men no shooting unless we call for it. Understand? We'll be in the camp. Your men shoot, they'll hit us."

"Understand."

As Thomas instructed the other Indians, Blancanales slipped on his equipment. Then Able Team led the force into the village. The Indians crept to their positions. For minutes, Able Team watched the soldiers in the camp.

Lyons nodded toward the boats. "I'll slip in along the riverbank, trying to get on the big boat."

Gadgets pointed to Blancanales and himself, whispering, "We get those Indian people out of there...."

"And declare a free-fire zone," Lyons concluded. Blancanales and Gadgets nodded. With a mock salute, Lyons crawled away.

They watched the soldiers. A fire burned in the center of the camp. A soldier held out a stick skewering a hot dog. He wore green fatigues without rank or unit identification. A Heckler & Koch G-3 automatic rifle hung from his shoulder.

A few steps from the fire, a gas lantern stood on the

end of a ten-foot pole, its unnatural white light searing away the constellations and swirling galaxies of the southern hemisphere's night. Another light on a pole was placed at the riverbank. The lanterns lit the camp like streetlights.

Two soldiers with G-3 rifles pulled a man from the cabin of the patrol boat. The prisoner staggered to the gangplank, steadied himself before descending. In the lights' glare, Gadgets and Blancanales saw blood on the man's face. Blood on tanned skin showed through rips in his uniform.

"That's the officer I saw before," Blancanales whispered to Gadgets.

Lurching down the spring aluminum gangplank, the bleeding officer staggered across the sand beach, then up the slight embankment. The two soldiers followed him.

A third slaver soldier left the patrol boat's cabin. He carried no rifle. He wore an ascot at the throat of his permapress camouflage fatigues. No rank or unit identification marked his uniform. A military holster hung from a web belt.

A dark-featured Latin with curly hair, he strutted down the gangplank, one hand on his holster, surveying the scene. He followed the prisoner and the other soldiers to the line of captives.

Shouting instructions in Portuguese, he pointed at the bleeding officer, then to another captive. One soldier held the officer upright, another jerked a captured Brazilian soldier to his feet. The teenager wore a single stripe of rank on his sleeve.

The dandy in the ascot shouted at the captured officer. The officer shook his head. The dandy unholstered a black auto-pistol, put the muzzle at the head of the teenage prisoner. Again, he shouted his questions.

The captured officer spoke quickly, strained against the grip of the gunman behind him. He repeated his words over and over again.

A blast rocked back the boy's head, threw him down. The captured officer stared at the dead teenager. He said nothing as the auto-pistol went to his head. The dandy shouted more questions.

"Is there anything we can try?" Gadgets whispered.

Blancanales shook his head. Keying his hand radio, Blancanales warned Lyons, "Don't. There are twelve prisoners we've got to get out of there."

"Pretty boy is on my shit list. . . ." Lyons hissed.

They watched the bleeding, silent officer shake his head to more shouted questions. The dandy kicked the officer's feet from under him, kicked him again and again. Finally, the slaver holstered the auto-pistol, strode away. He straightened the knot of his ascot.

Gadgets punched Blancanales in the shoulder. "Let's go before pretty boy comes back."

Blancanales led the way between the mounds of ashes that had been the shelter and possessions of the tribe. Checking ahead of him with a grass stem, he stayed on the footstep-trampled path. He kept his belly to the dirt, moved with slow caution. He saw the glistening monofilament of a booby trap. He didn't pause to dismantle the weapon. He unscrewed the fuse and dropped it.

A shadow lay on the path. Even with the light from the lanterns, Blancanales could not make out the form. Was it a soldier flat on the path, watching for Indian raiders? Blancanales flicked a stone at the shadow, then lay without moving for the count of fifty. The form did not shift or turn.

He thumbed the fire selector of his Beretta to three-shot auto and crawled forward. Passing a knot of weeds singed by fire, he spotted the small rectangular outline of a claymore. There was no trip line. But he did see a wire trailing from the back. This one was command detonated. Not stopping, he continued to the form. Finally, he saw a face staring at him.

Blood crusted the child's face. Blancanales saw no breathing. Crossing the last few feet quickly, he reached out to touch the child.

He stopped his hand. A fast wave of the dry grass stem found no wires or monofilament. Blancanales did not move the body as he felt for a pulse. Nothing moved under his fingertips. He raised himself up slowly and looked at the child. The opened lung and guts of the boy indicated a point-blank burst to the back.

As he crabbed backward over the path, a hand caught his boot top. Blancanales whipped the Beretta around.

"Pol! Be cool!" Gadgets spat. "What's up there?"

"A dead kid." Blancanales controlled his emotions. He started past Gadgets.

Gadgets grabbed him. "Why you going back?"

"Command-detonated claymore," he whispered.

"Forget it. I pulled the fuse."

Blancanales advanced again, skirting past the dead boy. Only ten feet separated them from the bound-back hands of the prisoners. Past the Brazilian army officer and the line of Indians, two green-fatigued slavers shouted Spanish obscenities at each other. A third gnawed on a roasted hot dog, watched the other men, grinning when the men shoved and grappled.

One man threw a punch. Blancanales slipped out his Beretta, waited an instant until the other man countered. A 9mm subsonic steel-cored slug punched into the first man's temple as a fist hit his jaw. The gunman eating the hot dog went over to the fallen man, stood looking down at him. The other gunman rubbed his knuckles, laughed. Then both men stooped down to help the fallen man.

Rising to one knee, Blancanales shot them in the tops of their skulls. They fell on their faces, thrashed. Blancanales rushed to the captured Brazilian officer.

"*¿Habla usted español? No hablo portugués.*"

"*No hablo español bien.* Can we speak English?"

"Sure can. Keep these people quiet. Don't let them move. My partner and I have to get all of you out of here before we can take care of these slavers."

"You're a gringo!" the bloodied officer exclaimed. "What are you doing in Bolivia?"

"Long story. Be still, we'll try to get you out alive."

At the other side of the burned village, Lyons stripped off his Atchisson, the bandoliers, the shoulder-holstered Python. He took off his shirt and spread it out on the mud. An Indian an arm's distance away watched as Lyons laid out his equipment on the shirt. Then he took off his boots, smeared mud on the white tops of his feet.

Two layers of genipap black made Lyons's face and body invisible in the night. He slipped his hand radio into his pants' left thigh pocket. Taking only the silenced Beretta—no web belt, no extra magazines—Lyons started away.

The Indian hissed something in his own language. Lyons glanced back. The Indian held out his hand. Solemnly, they shook hands, then Lyons continued away.

Light from the pole-mounted lanterns shone on the river and the ripple-lapped sand. But the slight embankment above the beach cast a shadow that paralleled the water. Lyons eased over the lip of the muddy riverbank and down to the shadowed bench.

Rocks and weed stubble scraped at his skin as he snaked closer to the two soldiers lounging against the windshield of the air-cushion boat. They laughed, argued. One man drained a beer bottle, threw it far into the river. Lyons crawled until only twenty feet of sand separated him from his targets. He took the Beretta in a two-handed grip and raised its luminescent night-sight dots to the head of a soldier.

Something tickled his nose. He reached to flick it away with his left hand, felt a slick, stretched strand of monofilament. Lyons backed up, squinted around him. A scratch of light crossed the shadow, continued ten feet into the river shallows. A large rock secured that end of the trip line.

One more inch forward and his nose would have triggered a blast of six hundred screaming lead pellets.

Scanning the shadows ahead of him, he saw the suggestion of a claymore's rectangular outline aimed parallel to the embankment. At his nose.

He had no knife. Testing the tension of the trip line, he bet his life the detonator was not spring loaded, that is, set on fire if an intruder cuts the monofilament. He reached toward the river end of the monofilament and pulled it. He slowly dragged the rock from the shallows. He crawled over the slack line and unscrewed the fuse from the booby trap.

Now, one soldier sat on the air boat, the other stood in the lapping water, throwing rocks at the bottle floating in the river's slow current. Lyons sighted on the heart of the sitting soldier. He squeezed off a single shot.

The soldier's mouth opened, his hand rose to his chest as he slumped off the prow of the boat. The other soldier turned to see his companion in the sand, not moving. He went to one knee beside him and shook the dead man. Then a muffled pop and the second soldier fell dead.

Lyons waited, listening, watching what he could see of the camp and other boats. He heard no one call out. The soldier sitting on the forward deck of the patrol boat still watched the river and the stars.

Emerging from the shadow, Lyons stood upright and walked calmly to the airboat. He dropped into the shadow beside the boat to drag a dead soldier to him. Blood drained from the death wound in the soldier's head as Lyons pulled off the man's shirt.

He donned the shirt and the equipment belt and slung the auto-rifle over his shoulder. A floppy hat pulled low on Lyons's head helped to hide his blackened face.

Lyons kept his face turned from the light as he walked to the gangplank of the patrol boat. His eyes scanned the craft. The soldier on the forward deck stretched, lit another cigarette.

The gangplank flexed under his bare feet. At the top, Lyons casually stepped onto the central deck. Several soldiers, their auto-rifles leaning against the benches, slept on the deck. Lyons swiveled his head, letting his vision slowly sweep the area. He heard voices in the cabin.

Each of the four men sleeping on the deck took a 9mm subsonic slug point-blank through the temple. Lyons leaned over the railing to sight on the head of the stargazing sentry on the forward deck. The slug slapped the man's head to the side. He splashed into the river.

Chairs squeaked in the cabin. Lyons pressed himself flat against the cabin. He saw a door swing open. A silhouette wearing a beret stepped out and walked past Lyons. The curly-haired Latin wearing the ascot stood in the brightly lighted doorway.

Perhaps these were the unit's officers. Lyons wanted them both. The soldier in the beret glanced at the four men who had died in their sleep, then leaned over the railing and looked for the forward sentry. The beret was only an arm's reach from Lyons.

Small splashing sounds came from the river. Both Lyons and the soldier glanced down. Flashing silver streaks darted at the dead sentry as he floated away on the current. One piece of silver attached itself to the dead man's uniform, thrashed and flipped. The tail of a fish arched above the river, splashed back.

"Piranha!" the soldier in the beret gasped, staring. He sucked in a breath, started a shout: "PIR-AN—"

A Beretta 93-R in his mouth stopped the shout. Lyons jammed the pistol deep, heard the soldier choke as a knee slammed into his groin. Lyons grabbed the revolver from the holster of the contorted soldier and shoved it in his thigh pocket. Then he pushed his prisoner backward against the soldier in the ascot. Both men fell through the cabin door.

Prone on the floor, the dandy reached for his auto-pistol. Lyons stomped on the man's hand, felt bones snap under his bare heel. Another stomp cut off the cry of pain. He went to one knee on the neck of the man, simultaneously grabbing the other by his curly hair and slamming the face into the floor. Then he stood back, his Beretta pointing at the two men.

Lyons whipped his eyes around the cabin, searching for other soldiers. He calmed his own breathing and listened. He heard no movement outside. A bright orange throw-float lay on a shelf in a tangle of nylon rope and girlie magazines. He jerked the rope down.

Magazine pages glided around Lyons as he tied the hands of his prisoners. He waved aside glossy pastel photos of breasts, thighs, bleached blond hair. Looping the thousand-pound test line around their wrists and arms, Lyons struggled with the tangles, finally losing patience. He cinched the tangles into the knots.

Turning off the cabin light, he crouch-walked out the door and scanned the craft's decks. He watched the gangplank and camp, keyed his hand radio twice, click-click, then twice again.

Blancanales answered, "Here."

"Where are you?"

"We're out of the camp. We got all the prisoners out. What goes on with the boat?"

"Five dead. Two prisoners. The playboy and another officer. Did you clear all the slavers out of the camp?"

"Negative. We cleared the camp of the Indians and the Brazilian officer. We counted eight or ten soldiers sleeping on the ground."

Shouts came from the cruiser cabin. One of the prisoners leaned out a cabin window, shouting to the camp. Soldiers on the ground sat up, looked around. They reached for their auto-rifles.

Lyons rushed into the cabin. The curly-haired playboy kicked Lyons in the stomach. Grunting but not falling, Lyons collapsed back, raised the Beretta, simultaneously flicking the fire-selector to three-shot.

Curly screamed as silent slugs smashed his knee. The other man went quiet, froze. Lyons sucked down a breath, lurched across the cabin. He threw the standing man onto his face, bound both prisoners together, looping the line around their ankles several times. A six-foot length of rope and a buoy remained. Lyons lifted the feet of the men off the floor, put the buoy out the window. He slammed the window closed, left the men with their feet in the air, the wounded man screaming.

A soldier ran up the gangplank. Lyons snapped a shot into his chest. Another soldier saw the first fall. He raised his rifle, looked around for a target. A slug punched into his head. He fell, his hand jerking on the trigger of his rifle, sending a long burst into the sand.

Other soldiers fired wild, spraying the night with .308 slugs.

Twelve shotguns and rifles flashed, a storm of fire scything down the slave raiders. From Blancanales. Gadgets. Thomas's men. More Indians from the village. Several shotguns continued pumping in double-ought balls. A pellet hit one of the lantern poles, toppled it. The lantern broke, whooshed into flame.

Two soldiers sprinted away from the attack, crashing into the jungle north of the camp. A claymore's blast—from one of their own booby traps—cut the two men down. Wailing came from the shredded men, the sobbing, quavery cries rising and falling in the background as Lyons keyed his hand radio.

"Got them."

7

Airhorn shrieking, the patrol cruiser approached the hidden tribe. Babies cried, mothers pressed their hands over their children's mouths, carried them farther into the jungle, away from the attacking slaver craft. The men and boys left behind by the warriors gathered their weapons.

Jamming a birdshot shell into an old break-breach shotgun, a twelve-year-old held the antique ready. The long-barreled single-shot shotgun stood taller than the boy. He pressed through a screen of flowering plants with giant leaves and squinted into the morning light flashing from the river.

His father and Chief Molomano! On the boat! Slaves! The *civilizado* soldiers had taken his father and the chief of their tribe. It was the end. The boy accepted his fate. He could only fight now and die with his people. Never a slave. Never.

Shotgun propped in a crotch of a branch, the boy waited for the soldiers. He saw his father waving from the boat. His father held the *civilizado* rifle of a thousand bullets.

Not slaves! Proud warriors returning from a raid! The boy shouted and danced and whistled. One of the older men nearby took the boy's shotgun, lowered the hammer and set it aside.

The naked boy ran to the river's edge, dancing and waving and jumping, calling out to his father.

Blancanales watched the children and women run to the beach. The men followed them down the trail, shotguns in their hands, flourishing the weapons to their victorious blood kin and friends on the cruiser. Their joy both elated and saddened the ex-Green Beret. He thought of years before, and half a world away, when Stalinist North Vietnam Army cadres had dressed in stolen Army of the Republic of Vietnam uniforms and called the people of a village out to receive free American rice. When the hungry people gathered, the NVA sentenced the village to death for collaboration and machine-gunned the crowd.

Those people then were not political. They didn't want war. They only wanted rice. But they died.

Looking at the villagers crowding on the beach here in South America, Blancanales knew they were like all the other peoples of the world. They wanted only to live, to eat, to have their children, to laugh sometimes. They wanted only peace.

But they got war. War with slave raiders. Cruel foreigners who took the young men and women to labor in a death camp, to create a metal precious beyond gold but without beauty, a metal invisibly resplendent, a metal valued for the horror of its touch, death by white light or lingering cancer. Here, the monsters killed hundreds. For the world, they plotted the murder of millions.

The people of this Amazon region had already suffered. But if he stopped the attack here—if he and his partners in Able Team destroyed the monsters and sealed their plutonium in the earth forever—then the suffering stopped here. The world would not suffer the greater horror.

Looking at the primitive, naked people laughing on the river beach in the Amazon wilderness, Blancanales was flooded with those memories and thoughts. When the patrol cruiser moored, he put his memories out of his mind and joined the people to share their joy.

Lyons cut the permapressed pant leg away from the smashed knee of the slaver officer. The Latin man's ascot now tied off his bleeding leg. Holding the leg still, Lyons poured bottled water over the wounds, washing away clots and debris. One slug had gouged the side of the leg, the next had shattered the shinbone. The third had angled through the knee, exiting in a tangle of sinews and bone. The slaver jerked and thrashed as the water streamed over his wounds.

Blancanales glanced at the bullet holes, continued his interrogation in Spanish. He held a syringe before the eyes of the prisoner, promising him an end to his pain if he cooperated. The Brazilian officer liberated earlier, Lieutenant Silveres, stood behind Blancanales in the cabin of the patrol cruiser. His wounds had been Mercurochromed and taped.

The officer listened to the promises and soft talk. After a few minutes, he lunged past Blancanales to grab the throat of the slaver. He shouted in Portuguese. Lyons recognized the word *Cubano*.

Easing back the Brazilian, Blancanales returned to the questioning. The prisoner stared past his interrogator at the enraged Brazilian waiting to kill him.

Words came in a rush. Making the sign of the Cross over himself repeatedly, the broken fingers of his hand purple and swollen, the prisoner gave Blancanales a long monologue. Lyons waited for a translation, got it.

"His name is Canero. He's only a mercenary. He has no political involvement whatsoever. He does what he is told. His patron is very cruel, and Canero fears him. His patron ordered him to find Indians for the work. Canero only did as ordered—"

Lieutenant Silveres listened, interrupted. "What he told you is a lie. I understand Spanish. When they thought I was unconscious, they talked in Spanish. They're Cubans from Florida. They work for a 'company.' Perhaps, like you, they work for the CIA. Nevertheless, I want this man executed."

"What are you saying?" Lyons demanded, his voice low. "You think this scum works for the U.S. government?"

Blancanales intervened. "What exactly did they say? Why do you think they're Cuban?"

"He said his girl came from Miami. She sent a message to him from Porto Velho. The 'company' would not let him go see her. He hasn't seen her since they were in France. That is what he said, then they tortured me more. Then he murdered my soldier. They must die, even if they are your—"

"Porto Velho's the city across the border, in Brazil?"

"Three hundred miles to the northeast."

Behind them, the prisoner listened. Blancanales turned to him, spoke to him quickly in Spanish again. Lyons watched Canero. He saw the man smirk as Blancanales interrogated him in Spanish.

"Hey, you!" Lyons shouted into Canero's face. "You speak English. So talk."

Canero shook his head. Lyons gripped the man's mangled leg and twisted it. Arching up off the table, he screamed, gasped, talked fast. "Yes! English! Yes, I am Cuban. I left my country many years ago. I hate Fidel. I hate the Communists. I am only mercenary. I fight because I have no job, no education. I fight only for money. Not politics."

"There!" Lieutenant Silveres declared. "As I told you."

"He's lying," Lyons told them. He gave the prisoner's knee a slap, making him thrash with pain. "Got to tell the truth, pretty boy. Or you won't—"

Blancanales shoved Lyons back in a Mutt-and-Jeff routine. "Take a walk, will you? This is my interrogation."

"Yeah, but I took him. I'll do what I want. He deserves it."

"It doesn't matter what he deserves," countered Blancanales, playing his part in the shove-and-lecture process. "This man is now our prisoner, and if he cooperates, he'll be treated decently. We won't turn him over to those cannibals out there."

"If he doesn't talk," Lyons threatened, looking at the now panicked Cuban, "then. . . ."

"We'll get our information. He'll cooperate." Blancanales escorted Lyons to the cabin door.

On the cruiser's troop deck, Thomas and two of his Indian shotgunners sorted through the captured weapons and equipment. A line of Heckler & Koch G-3 autorifles leaned against a side bench. Thomas checked each rifle, pulling back the cocking lever and looking into the chamber, squinting down the bore. His men examined the dead raiders' gun belts and bandoliers of ammunition. Blood caked much of the equipment. Bullets or double-ought balls had twisted a few magazines out of shape. The Indians carefully salvaged the undamaged cartridges.

Lyons saw the Western-style gun belt and empty holster of the second prisoner. He still had the revolver in his thigh pocket.

"Ironman," Thomas called out in his lilting English. "We take many rifles. Bullets. Very good war. You want food? Beer? The village now has party."

"Beer?" Lyons went to the railing. On the beach, Indians opened cans and packages from the raiders' food stores. They were sampling the exotic food, passing it around, laughing, gorging themselves. One group of children shared a pint carton of ice cream, not opening and eating it, but passing it one to another, sliding the sealed container over their never before chilled skin. They squealed and shivered, shook their numbed fingers. "All right, a party. And here's a present for you." He took the revolver out of his pocket and snatched up its holster and gun belt from the deck. "Christmas comes early."

Thomas examined the Smith & Wesson .38 four-inch barreled revolver. "But I am not Christian. Is not right to pretend only for gift."

"Pretend it's your birthday," Lyons said sincerely, moved by the Indian's openness. "What's a party without presents?" He bounced down the aluminum gangplank, the morning rays of the sun burning through his shirt. Filthy, scratched from the action of the night before, Lyons felt streams of sweat course over his genipap-smeared body. He rubbed his hand over his hair, used his own sweat to wipe away the crud on his face.

As he crossed the beach, children and women circled him, offering him a buffet of open cans: pork and beans, fruit, beer, tamales, tuna, boot blacking. He waved it all away, smiling, and searched through the boxes. Finding two cans of warm beer and several tins of sardines, he looked for an opener.

Tribesmen squatted in a group, eating and gesturing, describing their heroic deeds in the battle. They pantomimed aiming their shotguns. Seeing Lyons, they motioned him over. He picked up his unopened beer and sardines and squatted with them.

They wore new body-blacking and fierce bands of color on their faces. One man's face sported a band of

red across the black, with electric-yellow feathers
through his earlobes. Another had painted red circles
around his brilliant white eyes.

Lyons popped the top of a beer, keyed open the sardines. He ate while the warriors acted out the shooting
and killing.

A snuff pipe went around the circle. Lyons watched
the ritual. A man dipped into a flat tin of what looked
like Copenhagen snuff. He powdered a tiny crumb and
put it in the end of the reed tube. He put that end of the
tube to his nostril while another man blew into the tube,
shooting the fine powder down the man's nasal passages
and into his lungs.

Lyons had never seen snuff taken like that. It reminded
him of cocaine freaks snorting their drug. He watched as
he ate and drank and shared a can of fruit with the color-
splashed Indian next to him.

They passed the snuff pipe to Lyons. He hesitated, not
reaching for it. They waited. An Indian held out the reed
and tin. Lyons thought of Blancanales's instructions
when they had the breakfast of living larvae. He'd had
snuff before. He would live through it this time, too.

Taking a big pinch, he loaded the reed and put it to
his nostril. Sniffing hard while an Indian blew through
the reed, Lyons felt the snuff shoot into his lungs. They
urged another pinch on him. Again Lyons snorted.

A wave of light struck him. Blinking against the sudden glare of the sky, he saw every leaf of the rain forest
simultaneously, each speck of green to be a unique par-
ticle of a living universe.

"Hey, Lyons!" Gadgets called out. He shuffled
across the beach, a beer in each hand. "What exactly
are you doing with those dudes?"

"Snuff." Lyons offered the tin and pipe to his friend,
his arms moving through the air as if through water.

"Nah, I'm not into nicotine." Slurping beer, Gadgets pointed to the second of the air boats. "You know what that thing packs? That isn't any machine gun, that's a full-auto grenade launcher. And now it's ours."

Lyons stared at the mosaic of the trees. The Indians watched him, grinned to one another. Gadgets looked at Lyons, picked up the tin, sniffed it.

"Snuff? What're you talking about? This isn't tobacco. What's going on with you?"

A brilliant blue macaw flew across the sky. The sky and the wings became for Lyons one flashing moment of color, the colors and voices and pagan faces swirling around him were an overwhelming flood of sensation for him. His eyes opened as never before, he saw the life around him, savage and magnificent.

Lyons opened his mouth wide and let his spirit fly forth.

8

"Lyons is zonked. Put that in the report."

In the shade of the patrol cruiser's canvas awning, Blancanales disassembled and cleaned his Beretta auto-pistol. He shared the top of a shipping crate with a tape recorder. Gadgets paused in the report he dictated to reply, "He didn't know what it was. Said something about 'indigenous operations.'"

Blancanales laughed. "I don't know about that guy sometimes. For an ex-cop, he is strange."

"He's beautiful. But being a cop makes a man strange. It's the people he meets. The public."

"Put some Thorazine on the list. Isn't that what they use when PCP crazies hallucinate?"

"Don't worry about him. I asked Thomas about it. He told me Lyons'll be all right tonight or tomorrow."

"Sane or not, Lyons travels tonight. We leave here at dusk. We shouldn't be here now. The slavers lost a patrol and three boats. Today or tomorrow, they'll send another patrol."

"Gringos!" Lieutenant Silveres called from the cabin door. "Am I your prisoner, also?"

"No, sir," Blancanales told him. "You are not. In fact, we need your help as liaison with the officials of your country."

The lieutenant sat on the bench with them. "Why do you make a recording?"

"A report to our superiors," Blancanales replied.

"In the Central Intelligence Agency?"

"Why did you assume those Cubans were CIA?" Blancanales asked.

As the other men continued talking, Gadgets packed up his recorder and took it back to his electronics kit. He prepared the radio and tape unit for a transmission.

"Does not the CIA use Cubans?"

"There are many Cubans in the world. Millions."

"And many Americans, also," the lieutenant countered. "In countries where they do not belong. Where are my pistol and rifle, gringo? If I am not a prisoner, I want my weapons returned."

"Certainly," Blancanales answered, his voice smooth, smile lines crinkling the corners of his eyes. "We will return your weapons when we cross the border. Right now, however, you are in Bolivia. And it's not proper that you carry a weapon in a country where you don't belong, isn't that correct?"

"What? And by what authorization do you operate here?"

Giving his Beretta a last wipe with an oil rag, Blancanales snapped in the magazine, reholstered the autopistol. "This is Bolivia. We operate by the authorization of the government of Bolivia."

"Pol! Over here," Gadgets called out. "You got to help me run up this antenna. It has to go up this boat's radio mast."

"Show me the authorization!" the lieutenant demanded.

Blancanales went to the railing and pointed south. "You have to ask the man who issued the directive. You go upriver about five hundred miles, hop over the Andes, make a right turn at La Paz and go straight to the Minister of the Interior. He'll tell you all about it."

Over four thousand miles away, in the com-room of the
Stony Man complex in Virginia, the identification signal
from Gadgets's radio squawked from the wall-mounted
monitor:

"Good morning! This is Mr. Wizard, calling from
far, far away. Stand by for transmission."

As the machines automatically recorded the message,
Aaron Kurtzman returned to his makeshift desk with
coffee and lunch. Unwilling to wait in his own office for
the overdue transmission from Able Team, Kurtzman
had brought his briefcase to the com-room. Now he
heard the voice of Gadgets Schwarz. Dropping his lunch
on the table, spilling half his coffee, Kurtzman hit the
interoffice button on his telephone.

"April! Able Team reporting!"

"There in a second," the young woman called.

Electronically scrambled, transmitted to an orbiting
satellite, relayed to the National Security Agency in
Washington, then relayed to Stony Man and decoded,
the voice of Gadgets sounded toneless and mechanical,
as if synthesized. Yet his friends recognized his idio-
matic phrases and oblique humor. Kurtzman recorded
the report. April dashed in, took notes.

"We're about ten miles southeast of the Brazilian
border. Not that that means anything—everywhere out
here is nowhere. We have made contact...."

Throwing open the outer door to the pistol range,
April grabbed a pair of ear protectors and jammed
them on her head. She fumbled a page of notes, picked
it up. Before she had properly fitted the plastic and
foam phones over her ears, she elbowed through the
inner door. She saw Mack Bolan sighting his .44 Auto-
Mag on a fifty-foot target. Andrez Konzaki, standing
on his aluminum canes, watched from a step away.

Bolan was committed to constant practice with all his weapons.

The muzzle-shock of the AutoMag in confined space hit April's left ear like a hammer. She staggered slightly, and cupped her hand over her ear.

"Mack!" she cried out, her ear throbbing. "Why bother with bullets? Just point that thing at the bad guys, and let the noise knock them down."

Bolan smiled. He saw the papers in her hand. "What goes on?"

"Able Team finally reported." She passed the notes to the commander of the three blazing counterterrorists now in the Amazon.

Holstering his auto-cannon, Bolan speed-scanned the first page of notes, passing the page to Konzaki. The men read the pages for pertinent details. Konzaki took a microcassette recorder from his coat pocket and verbally listed the weapons and equipment requested by Able Team, "Twenty-five Remington 870s, Parkerized, plastic stocks and foregrips. Mag extensions. Luminescent sites. Twenty-five hundred double-ought buckshot rounds. Three thousand rounds of .308 NATO in H & K magazines. Fifty sets of load-bearing equipment, size small through medium. Ten hand radios. Rations, vitamins, medicine for one hundred people...."

Bolan sat back on the shooting bench, shook his head. "Leave it to Able Team to find the weird action."

"What did you say?" Konzaki slipped off his ear protectors.

"Cuban slave raiders—what do you think of that?"

"I think we should reserve an interrogation room at Langley. Put some questions to those animals."

"I've put out a call for Grimaldi," April told them. "When he calls back, if he can make it, he'll go south."

"We can't wait for him. If he's not available immediately, find a pilot down there who'll land a seaplane on that river.''

''And what about the inquiry to the Brazilian authorities?'' April asked.

Bolan shook his head. ''We have no reason to believe it isn't their reactor down there. They could be running the operation with mercenaries and crazies so they could deny it if it's discovered. Until we know for sure, I won't risk betraying our guys. How quick can you get those shotguns, Andrez?''

''One call for the shotguns and ammunition. One call for the LBEs, one for the radios. I can have it all by the end of the business day.''

''I thought they're on a reconnaissance mission,'' April commented. ''But this sounds like they're assembling an army down there.''

''Well, it's like this,'' Mack Bolan, veteran of hundreds of missions himself, told his favorite lady. ''It's one thing to give a good man instructions and send him out to do a job. But once he gets there, sometimes he has to do what is necessary. We've got three of the best down there. Three times over if need be, they will do what must be done.''

He looked at April penetratingly, yet affectionately, then shifted his eyes to the targets down-range as if contemplating the eternal shapes and moves of his war everlasting, and picked up the AutoMag again to blast some more holes with all the purity and precision of the cosmic balance itself.

That was Mack Bolan. Staying hard. The soul muscle behind Able Team's pulsebeat. Forever.

Your move, Able.

9

Wei Ho walked in his garden. Around him, captive birds sang in the jacaranda trees, the unseasonable lavender blossoms falling from the branches as the tiny birds—yellow, blue, iridescent green—fluttered from tree to tree. Recirculated water splashed over the rocks of an artificial brook. Behind all the other sounds in the domed, sealed garden, the whir of air conditioners rose and fell as the machines created the cool dry environment that Wei Ho demanded. When he drifted through the flowers and trees, enjoying the bird songs and the stereophonic classical Chinese music, he put the Amazon far from his mind, imagined himself to be walking in his garden in Shanghai so many years before.

A chime announced the arrival of Chan Sann and Abbott. Wei Ho clapped. A girl shuffled to him, brushed and straightened his silk robe, then shuffled away as silently as she had come.

Guards preceded the two visitors, stood at their sides as the Cambodian soldier and the American physicist entered. The heavyset Chan Sann stepped forward, bowed stiffly.

"Master, we have lost a patrol. Fifteen soldiers, two officers. One large craft, two hovercraft. Gone."

"How?"

"We do not know. Perhaps Indians, perhaps Brazilian army. The patrol had found a village. They captured several Indians for workers. Then they reported sighting a group of Brazilian soldiers. They captured the Brazilians, then we heard no more from them.''

''Where was this?''

''Upriver. In Bolivia. We have depleted the Indians in this area. We must send patrols to other areas to satisfy Mr. Abbott's requirements.''

''Send a small plane to overfly the last reported position of the patrol,'' Wei Ho instructed. ''If the river craft can be recovered, send another patrol. If the plane or patrol encounters organized resistance, dispatch a plane with gas. There can be no opposition to our efforts.''

''And if the opposition is soldiers of the Brazilian army?''

''Let no man escape.''

Chan Sann's square, brutal face never broke its mask-like composure. In 1979 the Cambodian fled his country as the People's Army of Vietnam routed the forces of Pol Pot. Sann and his Khmer Rouge soldiers had joined Wei Ho's personal guard in Burma. As they had for Pol Pot, the Cambodians killed without question. Unlike the American physicist Abbott, they acted instantly on Wei Ho's instructions.

''And now you, Mr. Abbott. More delays?''

The American shuffled forward. Years of heroin addiction had reduced his body to a gaunt wreck. Sweat pasted his thick hair to the sickly gray skin of his scalp. Sun scars marked his nose and sallow cheekbones. The preceding three days had aged the once brilliant atomic theoretician. He carried the stink of fetid mud. Wei Ho stepped back from the odor.

''They die,'' the American told him. ''I can't stop the dying. I thought it was the exposure. I rotated the work gangs. I kept the rem count down. But they died. Even the road gangs, the jungle cutters with no exposure whatsoever, they die.''

"Why does this concern me?"

Abbott reached for the pack of cigarettes in his shirt pocket, the action exposing welts of needle scars on his forearms. One of the guards rushed forward, as quick as a snake and seized the addict's hand in mid-motion. Abbott obediently dropped his hand. The guard returned to his stance at attention, watching every move of the visitors.

"I'm sorry...I forgot about your security.... My point is, how can you expect me to hold to your timetable? I don't have the technicians, I don't have the workers, I don't—"

"Chan Sann!" The Chinese leader pointed at the Cambodian officer. Wei Ho's never-tanned, never-lined face was a pale frozen mask. The cold, imperious expression like a warlord's, the black hair, the silk robe and the garden created an image repeated a thousand times in the old books of China. "Have you failed in your responsibilities?"

"No master. My patrols fill the quotas, despite the greater distances they must go to find Indians."

"Yes, they bring me Indians," said Abbott, "Indians who don't know how to use a shovel. Who work a day, two days, then sicken and die. Women with babies. And a baby dies in the camp and the woman cries and moans until one of your men comes and cuts her throat. And the Indian men try to protect the women, and after the shooting's over, there's a pile of dead slaves. What I want to tell you is that if you want this project completed, get me workers. Not starved Indians, not slaves—workers."

"That is not possible, Mr. Abbott. We cannot...advertise."

"Then it's not possible to finish the project."

Wei Ho regarded the American with calm, expressionless eyes. Should he have the stinking creature killed for his impertinence? Hacked apart, hands and feet then the limbs severed hack by hack until only a truncated flopping mass of screaming flesh remained? Unfortunately, no. Without Abbott, no plutonium. And until the drug-wasted atomic physicist completed the project, Wei Ho knew he must tolerate the American's whining. Even if Wei Ho found another scientist, he would not gain the secret of the laser separation of the isotopes. Only Abbott knew the process. Only he could lead the technicians. So the creature's miserable existence continued.

"Then we will find you the workers, Mr. Abbott. The project must proceed to completion."

After Wei Ho dismissed him, Abbott hurried from the air-conditioned garden. He restrained his body's drug hunger while the sheet steel of the inner security door slid aside. Stone-faced Chinese guards glanced at him through the bulletproof glass ports of their stations. One guard, his Kalashnikov rifle held constantly at the ready, followed a step behind as the gray, stooped American shuffled the length of the corridor. A second guard station, identical to the other, protected the door opening to the outside. Another pair of Wei Ho's personal bodyguards looked from their bulletproof ports and threw switches to roll aside the steel door.

Heat washed over Abbott. His expectation of the needle became urgent, sexual. Quickening his steps, he avoided the stares of the Cambodian and Thai mercenaries manning the perimeter of Wei Ho's compound. He almost ran to his Toyota four-wheel-drive land cruiser. Gunning the engine to life, he ground the gears.

The Cambodians inside the guardhouse sneered at the addict. The electric gate finally rolled open. Abbott stomped the accelerator to the floor and left the fortified compound behind.

He sped along the narrow asphalt road as far as the first turnoff. Swerving onto a dirt track, he drove a few hundred yards into the jungle. There, invisible from the main road that interconnected the several compounds, Abbott quickly tied off his left arm and plunged a syringe into a vein.

Abbott fell back against the seat as the heroin rush surged through him. A wind swayed the interlocking branches of the trees. Semiconscious, his head lolling from side to side, he stared around him at the lush growth that walled the clearing.

A living prison. Walls a thousand miles thick. Brave with the drug's strength, Abbott considered his future. He saw only death. He lived surrounded by suffering and despair and hideous death. The Indian slaves died of disease, shootings, whippings, loneliness and radiation. The technicians also died of disease and radiation and killed one another in drunken quarrels. The guards died in riverbank mud, ambushed by Indian bows and shotguns, sometimes died on stakes in the villages, mutilated, impossible to recognize as human. Death everywhere.

And now death within him. The cancer pain throbbed in his chest, always present. Abbott would die. The cancer ate at his lungs. He had no hope of treatment. The Chinaman would never allow him to leave for surgery and treatment.

So Abbott would die. Surrounded by walls of jungle and by death and by unlimited heroin.

Ah. The heroin.

10

Lyons returned from the jungle after dark. He wore a loincloth and black body paint patterned in red. He carried his fatigues and boots in a bundle under his arm.

As he crossed the clearing where the tribe camped, the women looked up from their cook-fires at the transformed *civilizado*. They smiled, gossiped to one another about the North American, continued flaying meat and turning it on their fires. Children clutched the fingers of his free hand, skipped with him on the trail.

The boats had been moved. On the riverbank, webs of woven branches concealed the airboats. The patrol cruiser was now moored under the overhanging branches of a tree that leaned over the river. The branches screened the boat from any observation from the sky. During the day, the Indians had lashed hundreds of branches around the rails of the cruiser. It looked like a sandbar overgrown with small trees.

On the beach, by the light of a battery lantern, Thomas continued distributing captured weapons and packs to his men and to the warriors of the tribe. Two of his men gave up their Remingtons, took Heckler & Koch automatic rifles. Blancanales sat off to the side and watched as Thomas and one of his men argued. The Indian gripped his Remington, pushed the G-3 away. Finally, Thomas spun to face the shimmering expanse of moonlit river, impressively fired burst after burst of .308 slugs into the night. He offered the smoking auto-rifle again to the soldier. The man accepted it, passing his pump-action shotgun to a village man.

Lyons walked into the glow of the lantern and squatted with the others. Except for his size, he looked like one of them. Blancanales stared for a minute, studying the transformation of the blond college-educated ex-LAPD officer. Lyons, still affected by the narcotic, wore his hair cut like Thomas's men, his sideburns shaved away, the nape of his neck shaved high. Genipap stained his hair, his face and his body black. Red rectangles marked his shoulders, like an officer's epaulets. A braided band of natural fibers held up his loincloth. Braided bands circled his ankles. He wore custom-made Indian sandals, new but already black with mud and body paint.

The Indian men glanced at Lyons when he joined them. Four men, who Blancanales knew had taken the hallucinogen with Lyons, grinned to their friend, then returned to assembling their gear. One Indian spoke with Lyons, and the two men bantered back and forth.

Blancanales watched with disbelief. Did Lyons speak the local language? Lyons even moved like the other men. He reached out, touched one of the G-3 rifles, his motions fluid yet deliberate. He ran his fingers over the cocking lever, the foregrip, the receiver, his touch on the plastic and steel looking as if he stroked a living thing.

"Lyons! Are you okay?"

Night-faced, his blue eyes like neon in the electric light, the blackened Anglo turned. "I'm great. How are you, Pol-li-tician?"

Studying his friend's face, Blancanales saw no obvious signs of drug intoxication. "You want some coffee? We need to talk about going downriver."

Lyons nodded. "On the boat. . . ."

Striding through the darkness to the boat, Blancanales followed the trail up the riverbank. He glanced back for Lyons, looked directly into his face. Lyons walked only a step back, silent in his thin sandals. Continuing, Blancanales heard only his own boots on the trail, the rustling of his Beretta's holster against his camo fatigues. He heard no one behind him.

An embankment sheered into the river water. The aluminum gangway spanned a twelve-foot gap between the vine-tangled riverbank and the camouflaged cruiser. Blancanales pushed through the mass of growth lashed to the rails. On the deck, he heard the gangway flex. He looked back again and once more saw Lyons a step behind him.

"I'm here, Pol. Still here."

They pushed into the cabin. Gadgets looked up from his electronics and locked eyes with Lyons. Gadgets burst out laughing, reached into his backpack. His Instamatic flashed.

"Hey, man," Gadgets said to Lyons, "you are spooky." He stepped back to snap a full-length photo. "Hope you had a good time today. Now it's time to work."

"Wait." Blancanales held Lyons's shoulder, studied his eyes, his face, his breathing. "Are you okay? You're looking weird, you're talking weird, you're moving weird. What's going on with you? What happened out there?"

Like a shadow of the street-cynical, rude Lyons they knew and loved, he looked at them with eyes serene, showing a half smile of amusement. "I am a changed man." He paused. "But we'll talk about that some other time, when we have the time."

Gadgets pushed a coffee mug into his hand. "Here. Caffeine. Get agitated. Then we'll know who you are. There's the map of the rivers north of here, where this branch joins the Mamoré. And we just got a confirmation and arrival time on the good stuff. An amphibious plane will come at dawn. Whatever our position is then, we radio them, they offload the goods and take the Cubans away."

"A spotter plane crisscrossed the river today," Blancanales told Lyons. "We don't know if they saw us, but we should be on our way downriver."

The weight of many men crowding on board swayed the patrol boat. Thomas called out, "We are ready! All men are ready!"

"Are *you* ready?" Blancanales asked Lyons. The black-painted loinclothed ex-cop nodded. "Then why don't you get dressed? You look radically indigenous, but it's time to work."

Unrolling his bundle of fatigues and boots and equipment, Lyons slipped on his shoulder-holster Magnum. He buckled on the web belt carrying the Beretta, hooked his hand radio's case to the belt. Opening his backpack, he put away his fatigues and boots.

Gadgets and Blancanales stared at the spectacle. Gadgets grabbed his Instamatic again, snapped yet another photo.

"I cannot believe it," Gadgets laughed. "Lyons, the Commando in a Jockstrap."

As the boats floated north with the slow current, Lyons watched the pale dreamscape of riverbank and rain forest pass. Above the jungle and gentle hills, stars swirled. The white fragment of the moon slashed the violet of endless space. The Xavante warriors around him sprawled on the benches or leaned against the railings, some sleeping, others listening, staring into the darkness for the lights of a slaver boat. But no lights broke the night whatsoever, not electric or wood fire.

No Indians lived in this area now. The slavers had de-
populated the forest, taking tribes for slavery, killing
whoever resisted, all the survivors fleeing their age-old
homes.

Purified by the hallucinogen and the rituals he shared
with the other warriors, the warrior from Los Angeles
longed for the battle. He felt loathing for the foreigners
who raped and killed and enslaved. They violated the
peace and beauty of this paradise. Now he went to kill
them. He felt honored that the Xavantes had accepted
him as a warrior and friend. He was thrilled. He would
not fail them.

He paced the boat, the new Atchisson hanging by its
sling, his hands folded over the carrying handle.
Machete-hacked branches and saplings lashed to the
rails broke the moonlight into slivers on the deck. He
looked back to watch the airboats, also camouflaged
with branches, trail behind them on the end of lines. A
plane might mistake the boats for a cluster of small
islands.

Spanish voices came from the cabin. Blancanales was
continuing with the interrogation of the prisoners. Two
Indians peered through the side windows to observe the
civilizados inside. Lyons joined them.

Blancanales questioned the second Cuban. The man
ignored the questions, said nothing. The first Cuban,
the knee-shot Canero, sprawled on a vinyl padded
bench, a field splint stabilizing his shattered leg. White-
faced with pain and blood loss, Canero argued and bantered with Blancanales, interrupting the questioning of
the other prisoner. Blancanales turned to him, repeated
the questions to him. Canero talked over the questions,
forced Blancanales to repeat the questions several times.
Canero laughed when Blancanales lost patience, shouted.

Lieutenant Silveres pushed a pad and pencil at the Cuban and shouted in Portuguese. Blancanales repeated his questions again, tapping the pad of paper. Canero spat on it.

Both Cubans laughed. Lyons had seen enough. Hurrying around the cabin, he shoved through the door. He brought up the muzzle of the Atchisson.

"Don't! Don't kill him!" Blancanales lunged to grab the auto-shotgun.

At the sight of the black-and-red painted demon rushing at him, Canero screamed. The other Cuban threw himself backward, trying to scurry to safety. Lyons jammed the steel muzzle of his weapon into the soft flesh of Canero's throat. The scream choked off.

Lieutenant Silveres kicked at the Cuban on the floor. The Cuban crawled into the corner to stare in silent panic at the painted madman.

Lyons said nothing. The shotgun did not waver. He picked up the pad of paper with his left hand, dropped the pad on Canero's stomach. But he didn't reach for the pencil.

The click of the Atchisson's thumb safety echoed in the cabin. Lyons held his gaze steady, half-lidded, reptilian, serene, infinitely cruel. Canero looked from the face of the demon threatening him, to the black-painted finger on the trigger of the oversize auto-weapon. He gagged, his throat spasming against the steel muzzle. Lyons did not take the muzzle away. He held it steady as the prisoner dry-heaved with fear, then vomited, sickly yellow fluid bubbling from his lips, spilling over his immobile face and chest. Lyons held the weapon steady.

Canero groped for the pencil, finally scrawled on the paper.

Only then did the 12-gauge muzzle drop from the

prisoner's throat. Lyons leaned forward, grabbed Canero by his curly hair, wiped vomit from the barrel of the Atchisson with the crippled prisoner's permapressed fatigues. Then, without a word, Lyons left the cabin.

Lieutenant Silveres laughed, watching Canero sketch a map of the city of slavery and plutonium.

Blancanales went to the door and saw Lyons pacing the cruiser's troop deck, his blackened body glistening in the moonlight, his hands crossed over the Atchisson. Blancanales keyed his hand radio. "Wizard. Be advised that the 'indigenized' member of our team is behaving in an erratic manner. Keep an eye on him, okay?"

"Can see him now," Gadgets answered from his perch on the radio mast of the patrol cruiser, where he had been scanning the silvered landscape with binoculars. "He's all the way at the back on the deck, talking with some Indian guys. Can Lyons talk their language? I didn't think he even knew Spanish."

"He doesn't. I can't figure it, either."

Gadgets called out across the boat. "Hey, Ironman. How can you talk with those guys? When'd you learn the local language?"

With a wave to the Xavantes, Lyons crossed the deck. Blancanales ducked into the cabin. He heard the steps to the bridge creak. He buzzed Gadgets. "He's on his way up. Be careful with him."

"Think he's flipped out?"

"He came in here, put that monster scattergun up against Canero's Adam's apple. Totally successful, of course."

"Threatening a defenseless prisoner with death? That's cool. That's the Lyons that Mack knows and loves. Sounds like he's returned to normal."

"Watch out...."

"Hey, Lyons! How's it going? Saw you jiving with the locals. How'd you learn the lingo?"

Lyons stood on the half roof of the bridge, looked up at Gadgets. "I don't know the language. Not yet. But they're teaching me. Numbers. Simple things. Hello. Goodbye."

"Hey, great. How d'you say 1984?"

"They don't use numbers over 100."

"Lights!" Gadgets put the binoculars to his eyes to see a boat round a headland. Spotlight beams illuminated the river's surface.

"A slave boat?" Lyons asked.

"Can't tell." Gadgets kept the lenses fixed on the outline of the craft a mile away. "Get below, keep them all quiet down there. Maybe we can drift past...." He looked down. Lyons had slipped away without a sound. Gadgets keyed his hand radio. "Politician! Boat ahead showing lights. Looks as big as this one."

"Lyons just told me. We're blacked out down here, staying quiet."

"Carl's moving real fast nowadays. Very spooky, in those moccasins and war paint."

"Come down to the deck, Gadgets. In a few minutes, it might not be safe up there."

"Down in a flash."

On the troop deck, Lyons gently woke the sleeping warriors, cautioned all the men to silence. Some of them went to the rail to watch the blazing speck of light approach. They spread the leafy branches screening the boat; they laid their rifles and shotguns on the rail. Gadgets came down the steps from the bridge.

"Can't get a good look at them," Blancanales complained, squinting into his binoculars. "Glare of the lights."

"Then maybe they'll tell us."

"What?"

Gadgets went into the cabin. Making a face at the stink of the vomit, he opened a window. Both Cubans sat tied, rags stuffed in their mouths. Gadgets switched on the radio, spun through the frequencies by the dial light, finally stopped on a band marked with a scratch. Only static came from the monitor.

"Lieutenant Silveres," Gadgets called out softly.

The Brazilian slipped into the dark cabin. "Yes?"

"When you were the prisoner of these scumholes, did you hear any of their radio calls? Was it Portuguese? Spanish? Did they talk in the clear?"

"Spanish and Portuguese. Once, a few words in English. Do you want me to impersonate their voices? I don't know if—"

"Not impersonate. You don't need to fake anything. Get on there, put out a distress call. If they answer, get their position."

Silveres nodded as he sat at the radio. He took a deep breath, flicked the transmit switch. His voice came in gasps, as if he were wounded, suffering. He spoke a few halting phrases, flicked off the transmit. Gadgets slapped him on the back.

"Supercool! You must be an actor."

"When I was in college, yes."

A voice blared from the monitor. Lieutenant Silveres listened. He held the map up to the radio's dial light. He nodded to Gadgets. "That is the boat of criminals. They called out the name of this gang boss, this Cuban." The radio voice called out again. "They search for the Cuban's patrol. Do we fight them now? I want a rifle. Or am I a prisoner? Tell me, gringo."

"Just stay here. We'll talk about it when we cross into your country."

"Then I am a prisoner."

Gadgets rushed out to Blancanales. "That's a slaver patrol. The lieutenant helped me pull a fake on them."

"They haven't spotted us yet."

Searching through the crowd of black-painted, heavily armed Indians, Gadgets found Lyons and Thomas at the extreme end of the cruiser. Thomas watched as Lyons loaded the boat's second machine gun, an M-60 on a pedestal mount. Lyons sighted on the distant spotlights, clicked up the M-60's rear sight.

"Mr. Iron! Down! That's most definitely the bad guys out there. Thomas, we have to keep everybody quiet. Maybe we can drift by in the dark."

"We fight?" Thomas asked, stepping down from the machine gun.

"Only if we have to. Maybe they won't see us."

"But they slavers, yes?"

Gadgets nodded to Thomas and to Lyons, returned to Blancanales. The approaching spotlight stayed fixed on the water ahead of the bow. Binoculars revealed lights in the cabin, silhouettes moving against lights on the bridge.

"We're going to make it," Blancanales sighed. "They're staying over on the other side of the river. As long as we don't. . . ."

Lyons stood behind Blancanales. "When do we hit them?"

"We don't have to. Luck's with us. We're going to make it past them."

"No," Lyons shook his head. "We stop them now. Here. There's only three or four men and boys with the village. If we don't fight now, the Xavantes' wives and children and parents are slaves, or dead."

"We can't," Gadgets protested, "go up against trained soldiers and machine-gunners with Indians and shotguns and some liberated G-3s. Brave, but not very smart."

"It's their families." Lyons glanced back to the Xavante warriors. Weapons left the rails, swiveled toward Gadgets and Blancanales. "The decision has been made. You with us?"

They looked into the muzzles of auto-rifles and shotguns.

11

The spotlight of the slaver boat swept over the water, found them.

Xenon white light splintered by the screen of branches cast patterns of searing brilliance and black. Shadows slid across the faces of the men as they watched transfixed as the gunboat approached.

"The mutiny over?" Blancanales asked.

Lyons took the binoculars and focused on the slavers. He squinted against the spotlight, then passed back the binoculars. "How can it be a mutiny? We aren't leading them. We're with them. Period."

Slugs punched into the cruiser. Impact threw an Indian across the deck. He groaned, sucking in breath. Someone put a hand over his mouth to prevent noise. Other men raised their weapons. Thomas hissed a command to them. They lowered their weapons.

Bullet-chopped branches and leaves settled on them. A long burst sent streaks of tracer red over Lyons's back. This was the slavers' recon-by-fire. Bullets punched holes through the cabin, breaking glass.

Silence. They heard the motor of the nearing gunboat and voices. Lyons saw the spotlight sweeping from end to end of the camouflaged boats. Not one of the black-painted Xavantes moved. The wounded man stayed quiet, only his gasping breaths betraying his pain.

On the deck of the slaver gunboat, soldiers held coiled ropes and boarding hooks. Other soldiers crowded the siderails. Two men on the bridge kept sweeping the spotlight back and forth.

"When they're up against us. Right up...." Lyons whispered to Gadgets and Blancanales, then crabbed away to Thomas. "All the men to the rail," he whispered to Thomas. "Keep them flat. Wait for me to fire."

With whispered instructions and shoves, Thomas and Lyons moved the men into line fast. Shoulder to shoulder, the warriors kept their shotguns and auto-rifles within the tangle of branches. Lyons took a position behind them and sank to one knee. He put an extra magazine of 12-gauge rounds for his Atchisson at his side and waited.

A steel grappling hook crashed through the branches. An Indian pushed it away from his leg. It hooked the railing. The cruiser's wood and fiberglass creaked as the soldiers pulled in the slack.

The cruisers bumped together. A slaver officer shouted instructions to his soldiers. Lyons put the Atchisson to his shoulder, screamed, *"Now!"*

Lyons swept a seven-shot burst of 12-gauge fire across the slavers, in less than a second four hundred double-ought and number two steel balls traveling at 1200 feet per second punching through the camouflage branches to shred the soldiers only ten feet away from him. At the same instant, fifteen other shotguns and auto-rifles roared from the cruiser. Lyons jerked the spent magazine from his auto-shotgun, jammed it back into his bandolier. He slapped in a second mag, snapped back the weapon's actuator. He held his fire as the continuous wave of flame from the Indians and Gadgets and Blancanales smashed into the gunboat.

Branches fell away, gaps in the camouflage screen letting in the blaze of the xenon spotlight. Lyons saw movement on the foredeck of the slaver craft. Suddenly the spotlight went black. The indistinct form of a soldier was swiveling the pedestal-mounted machine gun around. Lyons brought up the Atchisson and sighted on the man's torso. He popped a shot at him. Arms wide, the soldier fell back.

A single burst of auto-fire from the gunboat started up wild. Several Indians found the rifleman, hit him.

Weapons fire died away as warriors emptied their shotguns and G-3 rifles. Hands pulled 12-gauge shells from bandoliers, fed the tube magazines of Remingtons. Men with G-3s slapped in box magazines.

Charging from the deck, Lyons crashed through the sticks and leaves, his eyes and the muzzle of his auto-shotgun searching for movement. He hit the gunboat deck, slipped sideways and fell in the blood and shredded flesh.

A burst roared over him, muzzle flash lighting the gunboat's cabin door. Lyons pressed himself flat on the blood-slicked deck and with one hand pointed his Atchisson at a form crouching behind a flashing auto-rifle.

Recoil slammed the auto-shotgun's plastic stock into Lyons's forehead. He saw stars, but no form remaining in the doorway. Bracing his weapon, but staying flat, Lyons swept the cabin with a series of semiauto shots. Supersonic steel balls saturated the interior.

Fists hammered at Lyons. His Atchisson empty, he rolled away, pursued by one of the soldiers. Flat on his back, Lyons snatched the Colt Python from his shoulder holster and double-actioned a slug into the man. The muzzle flash froze the image of the crawling soldier lifting an auto-rifle from the deck, reaching for its pistol grip. His hand never closed, the .357 hollowpoint flipping him backward. He flopped on his back, his legs tangling beneath him. An Indian stooped over and put the muzzle of his Remington against the chest of the dead but still-moving man. The Indian fired once.

Walking carefully in the gore, the Indian continued past. Other Indians helped Lyons up, then spread out to search the gunboat for surviving slavers. Lyons crouched to change magazines, again carefully stashing the empty mag in his bandolier. Men called back and forth in the Xavante dialect as they searched the decks and bridge. Somewhere on the enemy boat, a man sobbed.

His CAR-15 held ready, Gadgets squatted beside Lyons. He eyed the corpse-strewn deck. In the blue moonlight, it was a slaughterhouse scene. Blast-ripped bodies, like bundles of rags, lay in contorted piles. Torn-away arms and boots, spilled entrails littered the deck. Blood pooled.

"Man, oh, man," Gadgets sighed. "Sooooo glad it wasn't me."

Blancanales stepped over the railing and came up to his teammates. "I don't think they even knew what hit them." He flashed a penlight on Lyons's face. "You're bleeding. You feel all right? Can you stand up?"

"I shot this Atchisson pistol-style, caught the butt...."

Blancanales turned off his light. "All you've got is a bump. That's other people's blood on you."

"We take one!" Thomas called out. "One soldier alive."

Several Indians dragged the man out of the cabin, gripping him by his uniform and web belt. Six inches of white bone waved from his right shoulder. Blood foamed from his chest and mouth. The Indians stood the dying man in front of Able Team.

Pulling a length of nylon cord from his thigh pocket,

Blancanales looped it around the stump of the prisoner's right arm, cinched the cord tight to stop the blood spurting from the artery. He eased the man to the deck.

The prisoner struck out with his left arm. One of the Indians leaned forward, a shotgun muzzle going to the man's face. Blancanales shoved the weapon aside. He ripped off the prisoner's shirt and examined the wounds.

Blancanales looked up to the others, shaking his head. "He'll be dead in a minute...."

"So will you!" the dying slaver gasped in English, blood frothing from his mouth. "Die puking your lungs, die of gas, you...."

Coughing and choking broke his words. Blancanales put his penlight beam on the man's face. He was middle-aged, with a long-ago-broken nose. The beam flashing over his body, Lyons's light revealed the sucking chest wounds, a knot of hanging intestines; on his left arm, web lines of scars.

Lyons leaned over the man and slapped him back to consciousness. "Junkie! Who do you work for?"

"Yankee *hijos de putas*! Wait for yours.... If the gas don't...the Chinaman will skin you alive, take a week to do it.... Me tonight, you tomorrow!"

"Who's the Chinaman?" Lyons shouted.

"Go to hell...." A gurgle of blood stopped the addict's suffering.

"He's gone," Blancanales told Lyons.

"To hell," Lyons said.

"A junkie mercenary working for a Chinaman," Gadgets mused. "Freaky."

Lyons aimed the penlight and closely examined the dead man. Jailhouse tattoos in blue ink spotted his shoulders and back. A faded *señorita* posed on a shoulder blade. On the left forearm, Lyons found words,

Puerto Rico Libre—FALN. He pointed out the tattoo
to Blancanales and Gadgets.

"A Puerto Rican junkie mercenary working for a
Chinaman in the Amazon. *Very* freaky," Gadgets
stressed. "And what about that gas he raved about?
What do you think?"

"Another boat!" Thomas called out, pointing downriver.

Blancanales lifted his binoculars and focused on two
tiny running lights. At a headland where the river
curved, a spotlight switched on. The xenon beam
searched the night, found the cluster of river craft. Two
lines of tracers arced toward them.

Lyons ran for the gunboat's pedestal-mounted M-60
machine gun. He slipped in blood, had to scramble to
the weapon. Finding a belt in place and the barrel still
warm from firing, Lyons estimated the distance and
spun the backsight's ranging wheel with his thumb. He
fired a long burst, saw no obvious hits. He called out,
"Thomas! Here!"

Passing the M-60's pistol grip to the Indian leader,
Lyons crossed the gunboat again and jumped the railings. He went to the M-60 mounted at the back of the
Indian boat, kicked aside branches lashed to the rail and
sighted on the spotlight. He jerked back the cocking rod
and squeezed off a burst. Again, because of the night
and the extreme distance, he saw no hits.

Thomas blazed away, arcing burst after burst at the
distant slavers. Tracers crisscrossed, slugs splashing in
the river, a few slugs punching the boat. Blancanales
and Gadgets circulated among the Indians with G-3
rifles, showing them how to twist the rotary sight out to
the extreme range, 400 yards. The riflemen fired aimed
single shots.

The spotlight went out. The slaver boat's tiny running

lights moved back for the shelter of the headland. The machine-gun fire continued. Muzzle flashes from rifles sparked from the dark form of the retreating boat. Then the lights disappeared behind the headland.

Firing died out. Thomas sent a last futile burst after the escaping slavers. Blancanales and Gadgets returned to the patrol cruiser. Blancanales paused to check the dressing on the Indians wounded when the enemy gunboat had reconned the "sandbar" with its machine guns.

"Anyone else hurt?" Lyons called out.

"Only this man. Through-and-through thigh wound, shattered the bone. He has to go out on the plane tomorrow morning. . . ."

"Thomas," Lyons called to the Indian, leaning through the screen of branches. "We get off the river now. We can't risk going farther."

"Yes, understand." Thomas shouted his answer, pointing to the headland. "Much danger there. They wait, maybe. Maybe many boats."

The engine rumbled to life, belching diesel smoke. Gadgets called out from the bridge of the cruiser, "In gear!"

Slowly, ponderously, the cluster of boats—the patrol cruiser, the slaver gunboat, the two trailing airboats—crossed the slow current. As they neared the riverbank, Lyons peered into the darkness, searching for a cove or inlet or island—somewhere to conceal the boats.

"Nowhere to hide, but I got a plan," Gadgets told him, as if reading his mind. Spinning the wheel, Gadgets steered the cruiser directly into the riverbank. The bow plowed into the soft mud. The gentle current slowly pushed the cruiser's aft around, reversing the cruiser's direction and pushing the gunboat aground. Now the camouflaged cruiser and airboats screened the gunboat from the river.

Lyons laughed, slapped Gadgets on the back. "The Wizard does it!"

"Not yet. We need a work party to cut more brush and tree branches. With that talk about gas, I don't want any plane spotting us."

Lyons nodded. He left the bridge, taking the steps two at a time to the deck. He paused at the rail to scan the open river for a moment, saw nothing but a long, shimmering streak of reflected moon. As he turned away, a shotgun muzzle jammed into his gut.

"Now, Mr. CIA Gringo, I am no longer your prisoner."

12

Surveying a topographical map of the area, Chan Sann directed his patrol boat's pilot to steer for the riverbank. By radio, he sent the hovercraft to a position immediately below the headland. There, the hovercraft's MK-19 40mm full-auto grenade launcher commanded the curve in the river. When the Brazilians came downstream. . . .

Chan Sann went to the cabin door. On the patrol boat's rear deck, a squad of mercenaries prepared their counterattack. Soldiers checked the belts of cartridges for the boat's M-60 machine guns, stacked ammo cans near the weapons. Other soldiers readied a third M-60, unfolding the bipod legs, closing the feed cover on a belt of cartridges. Chan Sann called out, "Hoang! Lopez! In here."

Two of the men left their work to join their commander at the map.

"You will take the machine gun and a radio to here." Chan Sann pointed to the top of the headland. "Our boat pilot will let you off now. You will watch for the Brazilians. Radio us when you see them."

Fear crossed the faces of the soldiers. Lopez, a Texan Chicano on the run for drug-gang murders, and Hoang, a Vietnamese-French Eurasian from the Marseilles crime underworld, exchanged glances. But they did not question or object to their commander's orders. Two men alone in the Amazon faced real and imaginary horrors. But to question Chan Sann meant certain death.

Nodding, they saluted Chan Sann, retreated to the deck. "Oh, Jesus," Lopez whined. "We are screwed! We got to go up there with the snakes and Indians."

Hoang looked at the moonlit hill overlooking the river. He tapped an American cigarette from a pack, lighted it. Taking one long drag, squinting against the smoke, he stared at the headland. He shook his head to Lopez, said in English learned from a thousand American movies and TV cop shows, "Who loves you, baby? Chan Sann don't."

On the bridge, the pilot spotted the riverbank and called down to Hoang in French. The two mercenaries shouldered their loads, Lopez carrying the M-60 on a shoulder sling, Hoang a radio and three hundred rounds of .308 NATO cartridges in link belts. As the patrol boat lurched to a stop in the shallows, mercenaries extended the gangplank to the mud beach. Flashlights, then the xenon spotlight swept the rain forest, revealing an unbroken wall of hardwoods and vines and ferns. The men remaining on the patrol boat stayed silent, their faces to their work as Lopez and Hoang descended to the shore.

Lopez stepped off the gangplank and sank over his boot tops into the mud. He struggled across the mud flat, the ooze and rotting slime sucking at his boots. Hoang followed a step behind, griping in TV English, "I tell you, baby, this is a bummer. A real bad scene."

Glancing through a bullet-shattered port, Chan Sann watched the two men thrash into the jungle. Then he switched on the shipboard radio and called to the radio operator stationed far away at the tiny airfield serving Wei Ho's city.

"This is Chan Sann calling for Williams."

"Complex Five. Williams speaking."

"We found the Brazilian soldiers at coordinates...." He read off a series of numbers from the map.

"The plane is ready."

"We do not know the exact position of the Brazilians. They hide upriver. We have set a trap. I want the plane to stand ready. I want you to ready a helicopter. Get ten soldiers. You will wait for my word."

The sharp circle of the Remington's muzzle cut into Lyons's gut. He felt the railing behind him, trapping him. Glancing quickly to both sides, he saw no one nearby. He tried to identify his captor, couldn't see his face in the shadows. Was the man with the shotgun the second Cuban? Or a slaver mercenary who escaped the massacre? Lyons expected no mercy.

"You will drop your weapons. First, the machine gun. Drop it."

Holding the Remington level, his captor stepped back. Light slid over his features. It was Lieutenant Silveres.

The lieutenant watched as Lyons very slowly, very carefully slipped the sling of the Atchisson from his shoulder. Grasping the barrel with his left hand, Lyons stooped to place the auto-weapon on the deck.

Lyons threw himself sideways and forward, chopping upward with the Atchisson.

The auto-shotgun's plastic stock knocked the Remington's muzzle up as the lieutenant jerked the trigger. A blast of double-ought splintered the railing. Rolling, kicking, Lyons dropped Silveres to the deck. He kicked again, the heel of his foot smashing into the lieutenant's crotch. Lyons scrambled over him to take the Remington out of his hands.

Lieutenant Silveres groaned on the deck, doubled up, his hands clutching at himself in agony. Indians rushed up, saw Lyons standing over the suffering Brazilian. An Indian stepped forward and raised a machete to give the prisoner a death hack. Silveres saw the black blade of the machete above him. He screamed.

Clutching the Indian's hand, Lyons stopped the blade. He handed the Remington to one of the men crowding around, then helped the Brazilian to his feet. Blancanales and Gadgets pushed through the crowd.

"What did you do, crazy man?" Gadgets asked.

"He wanted to escape. I didn't know he was a prisoner."

"He wasn't." Blancanales helped the lieutenant to the cruiser's cabin and eased him into a chair. Then Blancanales pulled the groaning Brazilian's hands behind him and tied him securely to the chair. "Well, he's a prisoner now."

"Finally the gringos tell the truth!"

"You are a prisoner now because you pointed a weapon at a member of our team. Perhaps you can explain yourself."

"And if I do not, you torture me?"

"Were the Cubans tortured?" Blancanales countered.

The young Brazilian officer looked up at Lyons. "By him...."

"I should have pulled the power fuse!" Gadgets blurted out, moving fast across the cabin. He checked the dial setting of the shipboard radio. "He made a radio transmission. Who'd you radio? Your unit? Your base?"

"Lieutenant," Blancanales asked the Brazilian. "Where is your base? And when will your soldiers get here?"

The Brazilian looked around at the three North Americans, Gadgets and Blancanales in camo uniforms, Lyons in the loincloth and body paint of a savage with his hands and body covered in crusted blood. Lieutenant Silveres clamped his jaw tight and waited for the torture to begin.

Blancanales sat in front of the young officer. He put his hand on the man's shoulder. He spoke in a soft, fatherly voice, "Lieutenant, I saw you when the Cuban brought you from their interrogation. I saw the blood. I saw him shoot your soldier, then put the pistol to your head. You told him nothing. I know I cannot make you betray your country or the other men in your command. But that is not what I want.

"Understand our situation. There is an insane terrorist operation on the border of your country. We believe its purpose is to attack the cities of the world. We do not believe this is the work of your government. But we cannot be sure there is no one in your government involved. Maybe one politician who has been bribed, one colonel or general who is in on the plot. We are not operating against your country or your nation's people. We are only operating in secrecy until we know the whole story.

"You may have compromised our mission, perhaps not. But we need to know what you told your unit. And when will they get here? Perhaps together we can annihilate the slavers. If your unit attacks us, then we all die, and the slavers continue murdering and enslaving Brazilians and Bolivians. If you cooperate, we can fight them together. What do you say?"

The lieutenant shook his head. "I...will...tell... you...nothing!"

Using a machete and the heavy barrel of the M-60, Lopez and Hoang thrashed through the vines and small trees choking the forest floor. Both men used flashlights, the brilliant beams illuminating the claustrophobic tangle of green enclosing them. Every few minutes, they paused in their hacking. They switched off the lights and listened to the jungle around them, black as the vision of a blind man.

They followed the gentle slopes upward and found the rocky spine of the hill. Low ferns and grasses covered uptilted slabs. No trees grew on the crest. Hardwoods and rubber trees walled the moonlit corridor of ferns and stone.

Soon they looked down on the river. The stone ridge dropped one hundred vertical feet to the water. The snaking channel curved around the cliff face, flowing from the southeast, winding around the series of hills, then curving again to continue north to the Brazilian border. Lopez and Hoang viewed an arc of the river curve from directly north to almost due west.

"This is Lopez calling Chan Sann. This is Lopez...."

"This is Chan Sann. You have reached the position?"

"We're here. Looking down on the river."

"Do you see the Brazilians?"

"There's nothing on the river. Nothing at all."

"Report every hour."

Turning down the handset volume to a whisper, Lopez repacked the radio. Hoang crawled to the drop-off and looked straight down. He scurried back to Lopez.

"Oh, man! Baaaad scene. Indians come, we are screwed!"

Lopez looked at the cliff edge and the ridge line of slab rock and low ferns behind them. He jerked out the M-60's bipod legs and slammed the weapon down. "We were screwed the day we got here. Loco Chinese, out of their heads—"

"Shut up! Hear that?"

"What?"

Hoang dragged on his cigarette and pointed to the river and the jungle east of them. "Hear it?"

Faint chopping sounds drifted to them.

"Yeah, like...." Lopez took the radio's handset, buzzed their commander again.

"They are coming?" Chan Sann asked.

"No, but we're hearing them down there. Machetes and axes and things. Chopping wood."

"Do you see the boats? Lights?"

"No, nothing like that."

"Report again if there is a change."

Lopez switched off the handset. "No bang-bang tonight. Those army dudes are digging in."

"If it's the army."

"It's got to be the army. Some strak officer who ain't paid off," Lopez told his friend. He took a belt of cartridges from Hoang and loaded the M-60. He pulled back the cocking lever to chamber a round. "It's either the Brazilian or Bolivian army out chasing guerrillas. Indians don't blow away river boats. One or two guys out wandering around, but not...."

"You got it, baby. One or two guys. That's us."

Lopez glanced behind him, eyeing the shadows and darkness, the impenetrable night of the tree line below the ridge. He intoned his words like a prayer. "There are no Indians out here. None. Not one. No Indians."

Working in the moonlight, the Xavantes chopped branches and saplings to complete the camouflage of the cruisers. Lyons carried bundles from the cutters to the men lashing the branches to the rails and decks. In an hour, the cruiser, gunboat and airboats aground on the muddy beach appeared to be only one more riverbank tangled with brush and small trees.

Thomas sent several men into the jungle to form a security perimeter. The other men returned to the boats. Only four hours remained before dawn.

Lyons went to the patrol cruiser's cabin and called Blancanales outside. "What has he told you?"

"Nothing. And I don't think he will. Lieutenant Silveres is waiting to get tortured. He thinks we're very crafty operators."

"We are."

"But we haven't given him any reason to doubt our sincerity. He's in a very awkward situation, but he's reacting all wrong to us. Like he was still a prisoner of the slavers. Like he's in delayed shock from last night, the shooting of that soldier. Today, I thought he was all right. Belligerent and pretty pompous, but I expect that from a twenty-two-year-old college student who thinks he's a career officer. I thought of sending him out on the plane, but now, with us expecting the Brazilians, we need him to talk to them."

"This morning he cooperated. When we questioned the Cubans."

"Then he demanded a weapon. That's when he got belligerent. Got worse all day, then he finally tried to take us."

They stood in silence for a moment. Around them, Indians struggled with can openers, gulped captured food. Others slept on the bare deck, their auto-rifles and shotguns in their hands. Lyons glanced into the cabin. He saw Lieutenant Silveres sitting upright in a chair, his hands and feet tied to the chair. The young officer was staring into space.

"Can't drag a prisoner all over the Amazon," Lyons told Blancanales.

"No, Lyons! He's a good kid. We can't. . . ."

Crossing the troop deck, Lyons took one of the G-3s collected from the dead mercenaries on the gunboat. Blancanales blocked the cabin door.

"You think you'll make it look like one of the slavers

shot him?'' Blancanales demanded, putting one hand on the butt of his Beretta. ''I won't let you. I don't know what that Indian drug did to your head, but....''

''Pol, the boy's a soldier. Watch.''

''What are you going to do?''

''Watch.''

Blancanales followed Lyons into the cabin, staying close behind him, ready to grab him in an instant. But Lyons's moves caught him unaware.

Whipping his knife from his gun belt, Lyons slashed the ropes binding the young lieutenant. He put the loaded G-3 in his freed hands. ''Okay, Lieutenant Silveres. We need soldiers. Will you help us?''

''Is this a trick?''

Lyons snapped back the rifle's cocking lever, once, twice. A cartridge flew from the receiver. ''There you are. I'm asking you, are you with us?'' Lyons extended his hand.

The Brazilian grinned, shook hands with Lyons, then Blancanales. ''We fight the foreigners together.''

Suddenly, all three men looked to the west. Rotor throb tore the quiet Amazon night.

''Lieutenant! Are those your people? Do they have helicopters?'' Blancanales demanded.

He shook his head.

13

An explosion of xenon and rotor blast descended from the night. Lopez and Hoang, shielding their eyes from the flying sand and leaves, watched the helicopter pass over them. Fitted with xenon landing lights and fiberglass pontoons, the Huey troopship hovered over the ridge. Mercenaries slid down lengths of rope to the ferns, forming a circle of outward-facing riflemen. Then the brilliance that bathed the hill switched off, returning the scene to moonlit night. The helicopter soared away.

"Think maybe there's some Indians who didn't see that?" Lopez asked Hoang. "Maybe Chan Sann should have included some skyrockets and sirens."

Their radio buzzed. "This is Williams. Where are you?"

Hoang waved a flashlight. One shadow broke away from the other forms, weaving through the rocks to the cliff edge.

Williams, a square-shouldered felon from the slums of London, wore no face blacking. They spotted the mercenary squad leader's white features from ten yards away. A black beret was tilted across his forehead. He carried an Uzi submachine gun.

"Over here," Lopez called out. "Watch where you walk, it drops off. Straight down."

"So where'd you see the soldiers?" Williams demanded.

"Didn't see nothing, man." Lopez pointed east, to the darkness and jungle below the hill. "We heard them chopping trees, digging in down there."

"I only saw one river boat when we flew over...."

"That's cause the other one got wasted."

"Blown away," Hoang added. "Way gone."

"Oh, Lord," Williams sighed. "You think it's the army?"

"Who the hell knows?" Lopez flipped a glowing cigarette butt off the cliff. "That's why Chan the Man's sending you down there."

"Great, just blinking great. See you later." With a wave, Williams started back to his squad.

"Maybe, baby," Hoang said as the ten men filed away into the jungle, their weapons and equipment clanking as they hacked their way through the undergrowth with machetes. "Maybe we see you, maybe we don't."

In the shot-riddled cabin of the gunboat, Gadgets's electronics covered a table. Wires led from a cassette recorder to the circuits of a slaver radio.

While Lyons, Blancanales and Lieutenant Silveres waited, Gadgets rewound the tape, then pressed the play button.

"Calling Chan Sann. This is Lopez." "This is Chan Sann. You reached the position?" "We're here. Looking down on the river." "Do you see the Brazilians?"

Advancing the tape, Gadgets skipped on to another exchange. "Do you see the boats? Lights?" the Asian-accented voice asked. The Latin voice replied, "No, nothing like that." Gadgets skipped again. The Asian voice spoke once more. "Find the Brazilians. Block their retreat." An English-accented voice pleaded, "You've got to get us out of there before the plane makes its run." "I will radio you...."

"That's what I taped," Gadgets told them. "The one called Chan Sann is downriver somewhere. I figure he put some men on the ridge overlooking the river. And the helicopter brought in a squad."

"And then the plane," Blancanales added.

"The plane will come at daylight." Lyons touched up his body blacking with smears of genipap. "Question is, with bombs or gas?"

"Takes a whole lot of high explosive to chop up the jungle," Gadgets answered. "I'd bet it's gas. Dig a hole, get behind a tree, can't hide from gas."

"Thomas told me about entire villages dying," Lyons said. "People dying with yellow blood coming out of their mouths."

Lieutenant Silveres listened to the exchange without comment. He cleaned and oiled the G-3 auto-rifle, watching Blancanalés sketch a map by the glow of a rag-shaded flashlight. Blancanales drew the curve of the river around the headland and pinpointed their position. An X marked the cliff overlooking the bend in the river. He put a question mark on the west side of the hills intersecting the river.

Setting down the auto-rifle, Lieutenant Silveres took the pencil and indicated two more snaking curves in the course of the river to the northwest. At the edge of the paper, he drew a zigzagging line.

"This is the border of my country, the Mamoré. The first town is 108 kilometers from there."

"Is that where your unit is stationed?" Blancanales asked.

"There is a garrison in Guajara."

"Is that your unit?" Blancanales persisted. "Will they have the soldiers to assist us when we attack the—"

The lieutenant interrupted him. "It would be better for you to discuss that with my superiors. I will help you while we are in Bolivia. But I cannot talk of what the army will or will not do when we enter Brazil.''

"Then a Brazilian force will intercept us here?'' Blancanales pointed to where the river from Bolivia met the Mamoré River.

The young officer only shrugged.

"Forget the Brazilian army!'' Lyons stopped the questioning. "That's tomorrow. The slavers will annihilate us—'' he grabbed Gadgets's wrist, looked at his watch "—in three and a half hours.''

"If we stick around,'' Gadgets said.

"If we cut loose and try to continue north—'' Blancanales pointed to the next bend in the river "—we get gassed. And we have another problem. Our plane will be coming in at dawn.'' He looked at Lieutenant Silveres. "And maybe the Brazilians, too. We can't off-load that plane in the middle of a three-way firefight.''

"Problems? We got no problems!'' Lyons buckled on his bandolier of Atchisson magazines and slipped the weapon's sling over his shoulder. "Who wants to go for a walk? We got the best jungle fighters in the world sleeping out there. Their fathers were headhunters and their grandfathers ate missionaries. Me and them are going over that hill for a rumble with the crazies. Want to come, get with the fun?''

Gadgets grinned to Blancanales. "That's our man, back to normal.''

"I'll come,'' the lieutenant volunteered, standing up.

"You sure, kid? I kicked you hard, you could be....''

"It was nothing.''

Lyons laughed at the young man's machismo, threw him a rag soaked in genipap. "Then black up.''

A hunter who had once lived in the area with his family and tribe led the North American and the Brazilian and

their Xavante allies along an Indian trail. Cutting
straight south, they followed the narrow overgrown
track, the hunter guiding them by memory and touch
through the darkness. Every man walked with his hand
on the shoulder of the man ahead of him in the line.
Lyons walked third in line. Several positions behind
him, he heard the lieutenant's boots crushing the rain
forest debris that matted the trail, his uniform's pockets
and flaps catching on branches and vines.

Night sky finally appeared above them as the trail led
up the hillside. By starlight and the light of the setting
moon, they crouch-jogged between the rock slabs and
low growth of the ridge. A clinking rang from a pocket
of the lieutenant's fatigues. Lyons called a halt and padded silently back to the young officer.

"You're making noise," Lyons whispered. He
slapped at the lieutenant's pockets. He felt keys under
the cloth. "Get rid of those! You don't need those in the
middle of the Amazon."

"They are the keys to my apartment in Belém. I forgot I had them," Lieutenant Silveres apologized. The
key ring jingled as it fell to the trail.

Lyons buried the shiny pieces of brass under the
forest mulch, then returned to his place in line. The
group continued in silence, moving fast.

An auto-burst stopped them. Flat in the wet ferns and
mud, Lyons listened. The line of Indians sprawled along
the trail, shotguns and G-3 rifles pointed into the night.
More shots blasted the silence, one rifle firing, then
another.

But no bullets winged past them. A hundred yards
down the hillside, in the total darkness of the jungle, a
rifle fired a last burst.

A soldier shouted in English, "Quit that, you dement-
ed fool! You're shooting at me!"

Lyons recognized the voice from Gadgets's tape recording. He crawled to Thomas and the hunter-point man. "That's the squad from the helicopter."

"We kill?"

"You think your perimeter men can handle them? The men standing guard?"

"If slavers come to boats. They lost in night."

"We want the two men who are watching the river."

Thomas and the hunter whispered back and forth. "He knows all the trails. We kill men on mountain, then kill squad."

"Maybe." Lyons keyed his hand radio, whispered. "Politician. Wizard."

Both men answered. "Here."

"You hear the shooting?"

"What's the body count?" Blancanales asked.

"We didn't even see them. That was the slavers shooting at each other. They're wandering around, shooting and screaming. You could warn the perimeter men. . . ."

"How?" Gadgets asked. "We don't know their language."

"Yeah, that's right. If there's an emergency, give them one of your radios. Thomas will give the instructions. We're continuing on. Over."

Tapping Lyons, the black-painted hunter pointed to the north. Thomas questioned the man in whispers, the hunter nodding. "He says we go take slavers. You, me, him. They close."

Lyons leaned his Atchisson against a rock and slipped off his bandoliers. He pulled back the Beretta's slide to chamber a subsonic 9mm slug. "Let's go."

Leading the way through the angled stones, the hunter moved like a snake, slithering through crevices, slipping through undergrowth without stirring a fern or branch to betray his passing. He carried only a machete. Thomas followed a body length behind the hunt. Lyons struggled to keep pace with him. He scuffed his knees and elbows; he caught his web belt on rocks. He reached into shadow and felt insects skitter up his arms.

After several hundred yards, the hunter stopped and motioned Thomas and Lyons to crawl up beside him. They sprawled on the high point of the ridge. To the west, black masses of treetops blocked the moon. To the north, starlight illuminated in grays and blacks the rocks and the wide river and the rain forest on the far shore. The hunter pointed.

A red spark flared where the ridge fell to the river, a glowing face emerging from the black. The amber mask disappeared, the cigarette zigzagging as the smoker gestured in the darkness.

"Jerk-off clowns," Lyons almost laughed.

"What?" Thomas whispered.

"We take them prisoner. For information. Is that possible?"

Thomas nodded. "Possible."

"Tell your man. I go first. And watch for trip lines, booby traps."

Sliding and crabbing over the rocks, Lyons closed in on the mercenaries. He heard their voices. He slowed, keeping his chest pressed to the rocks. He dragged himself over uneven stones, infinitely slowly, watching the phantom cigarette-lighted faces of the two men. A sharp stone gouged the skin of Lyons's chest, belly, hip.

One man talked in the English of prime-time American television and tits-and-ass movies; he had a French accent. The other mercenary spoke Tex-Mex street argot.

"I mean, like that Chinaman must be totally messed up in the head, loco, dusted.... This scene out here is total weirdness. Like I'm part Apache Indian. And what am I doing? Wasting Indians. I do not like this crap.

And Chan Sann the Man! When I see that dude, I see skulls. A world of skulls.''

"Hey, maaan, ssshhh. He could hear, dig?"

"Oh, yeah. Jesus. He gives me the shakes."

Flat on the small rocks and grasses, Lyons inched forward. One man faced the river, the other watched the river and the slab-strewn hill, his head swiveling back and forth, the back of his head to Lyons.

Lyons forced his limbs through a flat slow-motion crawl, sweat running from his body as he strained. He pressed forward, then waited, relaxing, breathing, listening to their conversation. He watched the lookouts as they smoked and bitched.

Only a body-length's distance of rocks and flattened ferns separated Lyons from the mercenaries. He slipped off the safety of the Beretta. With the fingers of his left hand, he found a pebble. He flicked it past the lookouts. The pebble hit a wide leaf.

"You hear that?"

"What?"

Another pebble skipped across an exposed stone slab. The mercenaries whipped their heads from side to side, staring into the night.

"Something's moving out there—put away that flashlight! You want them to cut loose at the light?"

Another pebble.

"Ohhhh, shit! I'm turning this gun around already!"

Hearing the scraping and clanking of metal on stone, Lyons scrambled the last few feet. He threw an arm around the neck of one man, pointed the Beretta into the face of the other man. The one he held was bucking and twisting.

"Don't move or you die!"

A black hole yawned in the pale circle of the seized

man's face as his mouth fell open, cigarette clinging to his lip for an instant.

"You speak English, mister?" gasped this man that Lyons gripped in a choke hold. "We talk, we help you. Anything. We the good guys."

"Thomas! I got them."

A few steps away, shadows rose from the ferns. Thomas and the hunter walked up to the mercenaries and began to search them. Lyons kept his arm clamped around the one man's throat, the Beretta never wavering from the face of the other one. The Indians found knives, a snub-nosed .38 revolver, tobacco and marijuana cigarettes, a plastic bag of pills.

Lyons laughed. "Did you come out here to shoot people or to party?"

"We no shoot people! We good guys, supercool dudes."

"You American?" the Latin asked. "I'm American, too. I'm Miguel Lopez, from San Antonio, Texas. That's Pierre Hoang."

"You're mercenaries, killing these people and their families." Lyons motioned to Thomas and the hunter. "You take them for slavery, you work for terrorists...."

"We didn't know that until we got here!" Lopez protested. "We're a thousand miles from anywhere. If we don't do what the Chinaman and Chan Sann tell us, he'll skin us alive. And that's the truth. For real. He's done it to guys. Skinned them. We've wanted to get out of here since the day we got here!"

"What do you know about the reactor?"

"You don' wanna go there. It's a death trap. Radiation city. But I'll show you where it is if you'll get us out of this jungle. This whole scene's insane."

"First, you take us to Chan Sann."

14

Chan Sann lifted the rifle to his shoulder to scan the night with the electronics of the Starlight scope. He saw a phosphor-green river extending into the distance. No boat, no mass of branches and wood, nothing moved on the calm surface. Every few minutes as he paced the deck of the gunboat, he switched on the Starlight's power, scanned the river again from the north to the east, where the form of the airboat waited in the shallows, then returned to the north in a long, slow sweep.

For an hour he waited, pacing the deck, scanning the river. His soldiers held their weapons ready to direct the fire of auto-rifles, machine guns, rocket launchers at the boats coming downriver. Camouflage or fire power would not save the enemy. The Brazilian or Bolivian army unit that had captured the two patrol craft would die in the concentrated fire of the gunboat, the grenade launcher on the airboat, and the M-60 atop the cliff.

But the enemy did not float into the trap.

At 3:00 A.M. precisely, Chan Sann radioed his other soldiers. He spoke first with the airboat.

"No movement at all on the river," came the report.

"Now lookouts. Lopez. Hoang. Report."

Static hissed. He waited, impassive, his thick Asian features like a mask carved in stone, his hooded eyes unblinking, focused on his thoughts. His muscled neck tensed slightly, tendons and veins beginning to stand out from his dark and flawless skin. "Lopez. Hoang. Report. Immediately."

"This is Williams. I saw them before I came down the hill."

"Were they in their position?" asked Chan Sann, his voice toneless.

"Hey! We're here. This is Lopez reporting. Everything's okay here."

"Why did you not answer immediately?"

"We...we had a snake problem...this black snake. It crawled up on us."

"Did you leave your position?"

"No! No, no, we didn't. But we had to deal with the snake. *Todo es bueno ahora.*"

"What have you seen?"

"On the river? *Nada.* Zero. We heard some shooting. We don't know who it was...."

"Report if you see movement. Williams, report."

In the mud and rotting vegetation of a trail on the hillside, Lopez and Lyons sprawled next to the radio. In the darkness around them, the Xavantes listened for movement around the unit. Lyons held his hand radio ready as he listened to the Cambodian question his other mercenaries. "Williams. Did you meet the enemy?"

"No. Not yet."

"There was shooting."

"We thought we made contact, but...."

"Go to the river. Find the enemy. Report when you make contact. I will radio for the plane."

"We're hitting them in the dark? In the jungle at night? No one'll know who's bloody shooting at who! It'll be total chaos! You'll gas us!"

"Go to the river, Williams. Make contact. When the plane is above you, mark the position of the enemy with flares. You will withdraw then."

"You'll gas us! We don't have masks or oxygen. If the wind's wrong, we won't—"

"You have your instructions, Williams. Obey the instructions."

After a long, static-scratched pause, Williams finally responded, "Yeah, good enough. We'll do it. But you've got to give us the time to withdraw."

"Report when you make contact."

In the darkness and stink of the slimy trail, Lopez cursed, "Jesus, Williams is gone. . . ."

"Chan Sann would risk gassing his own soldiers?"

"It's happened before. Williams saw it."

Lyons keyed his hand radio. "Pol. Wizard. Man in Black here. Did you hear what the man said?"

"But it won't happen. Over."

The line of Xavantes and foreigners continued downhill. As they neared the river, the hunter-point man had the others halt while he and Thomas scouted the last hundred yards of trail. Lyons followed several steps behind them, finding his way by touch through the darkness.

Splotches of blue glowed in the black. Lyons peered at the blue, saw phosphorescent footprints. He pressed his fist into the slime and debris matting the jungle floor. His fist glowed blue in the dark, a circle of blue remained in the slime.

"Civilizado!" the hunter called out.

Lyons followed the phosphorescence to the riverbank. The trees thinned. Starlight illuminated the rain forest, the muddy banks, the river beyond. Lyons saw the hunter motioning to him. Thomas squatted on a dirt embankment. When he heard Lyons and the hunter, Thomas pointed to the dark expanse of the river.

"The boat. There."

Three hundred yards away, the long rectangle of a

lighted window floated in the night. An amber streak shimmered on the placid, slowly flowing river.

"Can't get them there," Lyons told the other men. Thomas translated to the hunter as Lyons keyed his hand radio. "Wizard. The Man in Black again."

"What's the word?"

"Are these radios absolutely secure?"

"Positive. Unless someone has one of the three radios, the transmissions sound like noise from space."

"We got a problem. The gunboat's on the other side of the river."

"What's the distance?"

"A thousand feet, minimum. I'll have to pull a scam, get them over here."

"Wait, man. Listen, I've got the plan...."

Williams and his squad of mercenaries wandered in a lightless maze of mud and branches and vines. They could not risk flashlights or machetes. For an hour, they groped through walls of night-flowering vines and thorn trees, men clutching at the others around them, falling into slime, entangling their rifles and gear and arms in unseen masses of plants. Bugs swarmed around them. By touch and compass, they finally found the river.

The men flopped in a grassy clearing surrounded on three sides by forest. On the fourth side, the grassland fell away to the river. Bleeding from cuts and bites, soaked in sweat and slime, Williams stared up at the shadowy forms of trees and through them at the stars. After the darkness and claustrophobia of the jungle, the infinite depth of the night's star-shot dome intoxicated Williams. He sprawled on his back, cool water rising from the mushy grass beneath him. He sucked in breath after breath, thinking, scheming. *How do I live through this night?*

Fighting panic, he considered his problem. He swatted at droning insects, called out to the circle of soldiers, "Guttierez!"

A man slipped through the grass, silent, only a shadow in the night. Guttierez, a bulky Puerto Rican con who had worked in Europe, Beirut and Pakistan, crouched beside Williams, his rifle ready, his eyes scanning the dark tree lines.

"And O'Neill!"

A second rifleman struggled from the muck to stand up.

"Stay low!" Williams hissed.

"Stow it. No one's out there." O'Neill plodded across the marsh to them, his boots sinking with every step. The overweight alcoholic fugitive from Europe flopped down without a pretense of military posture.

"This is it," said Williams. "Chan Sann wants us to hit whoever's got those boats—Brazilians, rubber workers, who the hell. We bang away at them until the plane gets here. Then we mark them with flares, pull back, the plane does the gasser on them."

"With the chlorine gas? We'll be down here!" O'Neill lurched to one knee and grabbed Williams's uniform. "Radio him, beg him—stop the plane...."

Guttierez slapped down the man's hands. "Can we mark them with grenades?" asked the Puerto Rican.

"My thoughts exactly. Open up your kits. Let's have a look at exactly what you've got."

Shrugging off his pack, Guttierez pulled back the top flap. He felt through the carefully packaged contents and found five fiberboard tubes. Each contained a rifle grenade. Guttierez used his body as a shield while Williams waved a penlight over the printing on the tubes.

"Yellow flare...two-second duration...parachute

pops at 100 meters. No good. Red flare...same thing. High explosive, range 350 meters, now that's more like it. What about you, O'Neill? I put five flares in your load.''

The florid boozer spilled out his backpack. Plastic sheeting, tangled cords, spare magazines for his G-3 littered the grass. ''Flares? I don't know if...don't think that....''

Williams and Guttierez tore through the clutter. Guttierez backhanded O'Neill, the slap like a pistol shot in the silence. *''Chinga! Maricón!''*

''You rummy bastard!'' spat Williams. ''Where are they? I gave you ten grenades and flares to carry. It was your bloody duty!''

''We never used any before....'' O'Neill whined as fists hammered his face. He scrambled away. Not content with beating the alcoholic, Guttierez jerked out his auto-pistol. O'Neill shrieked, ran away. Williams pushed the pistol to the sky.

''You want to broadcast our position?''

Guttierez lowered the pistol's hammer and returned the weapon to his holster. *''Eso gusano es muerto.''*

''Kill him in the daylight. Right now, go to every man, get any rifle flares he has....''

Without a word, Guttierez slunk away and moved unseen through the low grass. He went to every man in the defensive circle. He visited O'Neill, punching him several more times.

Williams examined the flares. Made for NATO, the projectiles had tails and fins that slipped over the muzzles of G-3 rifles. Firing a bullet from the rifle propelled the flare or grenade. A grenade had a range of about 350 yards. A flare flew a little more than 100 yards before its mini-parachute popped out. The flare then burned two seconds as it floated down.

Returning stealthily, Guttierez laid down four more

packing tubes in front of Williams. "What will you do?"

"Watch." Williams jammed the point of his bayonet through the aluminum nose of a flare and pried the end away. Pulling a tiny white parachute from the flare housing, he cut the lines.

In the cabin of the captured gunboat, Gadgets adjusted the antenna of a slaver radio. The voices of Williams and Chan Sann spoke from the radio.

"We think we've spotted them. There are lights and voices coming from a riverbank. We'll close the distance, report back before we open fire."

"Good. I will radio the plane."

The voices cut off as the Cambodian changed radios. Gadgets keyed his hand radio. "Pol. They saw the flashlights. The squad's coming in."

"Ready to move," Blancanales answered.

Voices blared from the monitor again. "This is Chan Sann on the river, calling Complex Five. Complex Five."

"This is the airstrip. The plane is ready. The pilot is here, waiting."

"There can be no delays. Have the pilot check the bombs, then start the engine. It must be here five minutes after I radio."

"Yes, sir. I will relay the instructions."

"Have the pilot report to me on this frequency when he is ready."

Gadgets laughed as he keyed his hand radio. "Man in Black, the plan's in motion. Politician, make your motions!"

"Ready and able."

Flat in the mud, Williams inched forward. Guttierez crawled beside him in the riverbank slime. They pushed through clumps of riverweeds, eased through shallows.

Two hundred fifty yards of beach and low brush separated them from the lights and voices. Fifty yards more, then he would radio Chan Sann....

Panic no longer clutched Williams. He had a good chance of surviving the bombing of the Brazilians. There was no wind to fan the chlorine gas. And modifying the rifle flares gave him another hundred yards of safety margin. And if the nine men behind them held their fire until he and Guttierez launched the first flares.... And if....

Disregarding the psychotic Cambodian's instructions for his squad to attack the intruders, then mark the target with flares for the plane overhead, Williams would wait to hear the plane before launching the first flare. His squad would then cover the retreat of himself and Guttierez. The Englishman hoped to have 300 yards of open ground between him and the Brazilians before the canisters of liquid chlorine and high explosive found their targets.

"A soldier's first duty is to live through it," his old dad always told him. Williams intended to survive this night.

Ahead of them, a very slight rise blacked the lights. Williams scurried up the hard-packed mud and raised his head. In the distance, a light waved over a stand of trees. The sound of machetes came to him. Guttierez snaked over the rise. Williams followed him.

Hands took him. He felt a knife at his throat, a pistol against his skull. To his side, Guttierez thrashed.

"Don't move and you live. We're enemies of Chan Sann. Not you. We don't want to kill you."

A man fell across them. Guttierez tried to bring up his G-3. The slash of a machete took away the Puerto Rican's right arm, his head snapping back simultaneously as three subsonic 9mm slugs slammed into his right eye and forehead. He fell backward.

The hot pistol returned to Williams's head. "He's dead. You can live. Help us kill Chan Sann, and you get out of the Amazon alive."

Williams went slack in their grip and surrendered.

The drone of a piston engine approached from the east. Mercenaries crowded the rails of the gunboat to watch the Cessna cross the night sky above them, its silhouette a black X on the stars. Chan Sann peered at the plane 1000 feet above the river. He returned to the gunboat's cabin and radioed Williams.

"Prepare to mark the enemy's position. Acknowledge."

The reports of auto-rifles blasted from the walkie-talkie's tiny speaker. "Immediately. We'll hit—"

Electronic roar overwhelmed the frequency. Chan Sann clicked the walkie-talkie's transmit key again and again. But the static roared from the monitor of the shipboard radio also. He hit the console of the radio with the flat of his hand. The monitor crackled, but the noise continued. The disturbance had cut his communications with both Williams and the pilot of the plane.

Rectangles of white light traveled around the interior of the cabin. Chan Sann squinted against the sudden glare. Light more brilliant than the noonday sun arced across the night.

"Commander Chan!" the pilot called down to him. "Flares from the shore!"

"What?"

Rushing across the deck, Chan Sann pushed through the mercenaries at the rails. He heard and saw red tracers streak from the far bank of the river and rake the location of the airboat. The sounds of a firefight ripped the night. Then the searing white light of a magnesium flare streaked toward them.

Panic took the group of soldiers. A squad leader clicked his hand radio and shouted into the microphone. Other soldiers ran into the cabin, hands flipped the on-board radio's transmit key. When they heard only the roaring static, the men slammed the radio with their fists.

"The gas plane's coming in!" a mercenary screamed.

A canister tumbled down, end over end from the belly of the Cessna. The men stood transfixed at the sight, watching their death drop toward them. The canister hit the water twenty yards from the gunboat and popped as the small explosive charge burst the tank of liquid chlorine. A ball of yellow gas churned over the river.

Chan Sann returned to the cabin. "Out! All of you, out!" he ordered the men crowding around the radio console.

The boat's diesel engine chugged. The pilot started the engine, revving it.

"It's making another run!" a voice shouted from the deck as the gunboat moved, and the drone of the plane returned.

Jerking ports closed, Chan Sann raced the gas. Outside, a man choked. A man rushed into the cabin, gasping, his eyes streaming fluid as chlorine attacked the delicate tissues of his corneas and mucous membranes. Chan Sann shoved him outside. There wouldn't be space or oxygen for all the men in the cabin. And Chan Sann had only one gas mask.

Another man struggled through the small doorway. Chan Sann pulled his Browning 9mm automatic and fired point-blank into the soldier's face. He fired four more unaimed slugs into the men behind the dead soldier, then slammed the door closed. He threw the bolt and dragged a steel chest across the doorway.

Screams came from the deck. Chan Sann slipped on

his mask as he heard the plane pass low. A second canister exploded less than twenty feet away, a wave of water and metal fragments hitting the gunboat.

Crowded with dying men, the gunboat began to drift aimlessly downstream.

15

As the last minutes of night grayed to day, Blancanales poured buckets of chill river water over Lyons. Filthy and naked, Lyons stood shivering on a sand beach. Mist blanketed the sand and the mirror-calm river. Hundred-foot tapestries of shadowy forest rose from the far bank. Dawn light broke through the highest branches, the shattered radiance beaming shafts over the mist that shrouded the river and its beaches.

Lyons grabbed handfuls of sand to scrub away blood and diesel oil and jungle slime. His genipap dissolved to reveal his sun-browned body. Scrubbing his waist and buttocks and legs exposed the white band left by the stretch trunks he usually wore to beaches.

Higher on the sandy slope, Gadgets sprawled on his poncho with the shortwave radio, monitoring a band to the pilot of the Stony Man seaplane. The plane approached. They had received their first communication from the pilot thirty minutes before. Now they waited for the sound of the engines.

The radio blared. "This is the Bird. Coming in on your signal. See a river."

"Can't hear your engines yet...."

In the west, the three men of Able Team heard a buzz. Their heads turned simultaneously. The noise grew louder. Only seconds later, the props of the two-engined seaplane ripped the gray silence, the plane passing low over the rain forest. Morning light flashed from the plane's wings as it soared in a wide banking loop, the pilot reversing direction to land with the rising sun behind him.

"This is Hardman Three," Gadgets shouted into the radio. "We're around the bend two or three hundred yards from the boats. We got a crowd of prisoners, and we don't want all of them seeing our team and you pilots in the daylight. So go on past the boats. We'll offload down here. Got it?"

"Read you loud and clear. Touching down now."

The roar returned as the seaplane descended. They lost sight of it behind the bend, then it appeared again, skimming low, its pontoons finally slicing the misted water. Prop blast foamed the river.

The seaplane pivoted on its pontoons and approached the shore. The engines died. Blancanales dumped a last bucket of water over Lyons's head. Voices rang out as Indians ran from the camp, their bare feet and sandals slapping the sand. Warriors carried the stretchers of the Indians wounded from the "recon-by-fire" the night before, plus the knee-shot Cuban pretty boy. Others herded the second captive Cuban. Lieutenant Silveres jogged with them, his H&K G-3 slung over his shoulder.

Lyons knotted his waistband and pulled his loincloth tight. He waited with Blancanales as the plane eased up to the beach, its pontoons scraping on small rocks. The pilot switched off the engines. A side door flew open.

Crowding around the door, the Indians received crates and packages. Thomas organized the men into a line. Pairs of men lugged rope-handled crates to the sand. Other men carried plastic-wrapped packages. Stenciled words identified the contents: Canned Meat, Vitamins, Medical. In minutes, crates and wooden boxes and packages covered the beach.

Splashing through the shallows, Lyons and Blancanales peered in the side door. Blancanales shouted over the chatter and laughter, "Any special instructions?"

A pilot looked up from unlashing a stack of crates. It was the copilot of the DC-3 from three nights before.

"Well, say. How you all doing here? Looks like you're making friends and influencing people." He stared at Lyons. "Looks like you lost your soldier suit."

"What about messages?" Blancanales repeated.

"Maybe next time. This is the last of it. Now where are my passengers?"

The copilot shoved three more crates to the door. Indians took two, Blancanales and Lyons the third, a box marked Radios. Several Indians heaved the second Cuban into the plane. Then the stretcher men loaded the wounded aboard.

"Those Cubans give you any trouble," Lyons called out, "tell them to take a walk!"

"Will do!" the copilot laughed. With a salute, he jerked the door closed.

Starters whined inside the engines. All the men retreated from the plane. The engines roared to life, throwing spray as the seaplane maneuvered. In the center of the river, the engines shrieked with maximum rpm and the plane soared away.

Silence returned to the forest. In the distance, birds whistled and cried out. Insects droned. On the beach, Gadgets sorted the cargo. Lieutenant Silveres surveyed the equipment and provisions.

"Weapons. Ammunition. For many more men and much more fighting. You must tell me now what you intend. My country is only eight or nine kilometers from this place."

Gadgets called out to his partners. "Hey, over here. The lieutenant wants a briefing." Lyons and Blancanales joined them.

"Do you continue into my country?"

"What we have to do," Lyons said, "is to get out of here before the slavers send another plane to gas us. We need to make distance."

"I ask you again," the lieutenant's voice rose with impatience. "Do you continue into my country?"

Able Team did not answer. Blancanales glanced to Lyons and Gadgets, finally nodded an answer. Yes.

"You say you have a directive from *this* country," the lieutenant said. "But by what authorization will you invade *my* country?"

"Perhaps," Blancanales grinned, speaking softly, calmly, "we can speak to your superiors later today. Where do they wait for us? We will meet and discuss—"

"Do not joke with me, gringo!" the lieutenant jerked the G-3 auto-rifle from his shoulder.

Blancanales had Silveres by the throat in an instant, kicking the officer's feet from under him to dump him flat on his back in the sand. He put a knee into his chest, screamed down into the young man's face, "Don't you ever call me that again! My first language was Spanish. I grew up in the barrio. I had to learn English in school. If it's anyone here who's a gringo, it's you. With your arrogance and petty, pompous macho.... You stupid little college punk—you must really think you're blessed by God."

"Wow, Lieutenant," Gadgets laughed, "you live dangerous. I never saw anyone get the Pol pissed. You got life insurance?"

"What are we going to do with him?" Blancanales asked, standing. He helped Lieutenant Silveres to his feet, slapping sand from his uniform. He picked up the G-3 and shook sand from it, then returned it to the young officer. "Really, we have to come to an understanding with you, Lieutenant."

"I thought we had an understanding," Lyons stepped up, buckling his Python's shoulder holster. "We need soldiers, we need allies. We'll need your help today or tomorrow, but all you're doing is giving us trouble. Can't you trust us for a day or two?"

"Do you think it so strange that I defend my country?" the lieutenant asked.

Exasperated, Blancanales shook his head. Finally, he spoke slowly, with fatherly patience. "Lieutenant, if we were the enemies of your country, would you be alive now?"

"The United States said it was the friend of Argentina, then betrayed Argentina to the British Imperialists."

Lyons stopped the argument. "This punk's a dunce. He does not understand the real world of Mack Bolan. For the sake of the survival of good and gentle people, we have to explain it to him. But let me keep it simple. Here it is. Step out of line again—like last night, like this morning—you die. No talk, no philosophy. A bullet. Understand? No, don't answer. We don't have time to hear it. Thomas! Assemble the men!"

They divided their force into two groups. A small group of men escorted the mercenary prisoners back to the tribe. The prisoners marched in a line, a long rope linking their necks. They carried loads of food, medicine and weapons for the people. In a few days, Thomas promised the defeated mercenaries, planes would take them out of the Amazon. Though many of them faced extradition and trial for crimes in other nations of the world, the mercenaries cheered their fate. They preferred any prison in the world to horror and death from Chan Sann.

The main force crossed the river, then camouflaged the cruisers. They continued north overland. Able Team and the Xavante warriors carried loads, also. As they expected to recruit more fighters en route to the slaver camps, every Indian carried extra weapons lashed to their new green-patterned packs. The made-in-Taiwan load-bearing equipment bulged with H&K magazines and boxes of 12-gauge double-ought. A team of Indian warriors carried the group's only heavy weapon, an M-60 machine gun and a thousand rounds of belted cartridges. Weight and the lack of tripods for the gunboat weapons—the other M-60s and the full-auto 40mm grenade launchers—forced the fighters to leave the other weapons behind.

Zigzagging up a ridge of hills, they reached the crest as the day's temperature became intolerable. A heat-scorched ridge line viewed the snaking river to the south and west. To the north and east, another river shimmered in the blazing sunlight: the Mamoré River, the natural boundary of Rondônia, one of the western states of Brazil. The Mamoré coursed northwest and joined the Madeira, the waters of the Andes finally draining into the Atlantic Ocean.

"Take a break!" Gadgets gasped, stooped under the weight of his radios and electronics. He ignored the panorama, collapsing in a tangle of leaves and grasses.

"By the map," Blancanales told them, "if we push all day, we'll make the Mamoré with one or two hours of daylight left."

Gadgets jumped up shrieking. A mass of thousand-footed worms covered his pack and clothes. Flailing at the millipedes, he hopped about in distress. Lyons pulled off Gadgets's backpack and swept the crawling insects from his collar, brushing them out of his hair.

Whipping off his sweat-soaked cameo shirt, Gadgets finally shook off the last of the millipedes. The Indians around them laughed at the North Americans' antics.

With a glance at the map, Lyons pulled his poncho out

of his pack. "Forget it. I haven't slept in three nights."

Lyons sat and closed his eyes.

He opened them as someone shook him. He blinked at the afternoon shadows around him. In only an instant, the sun had dropped in the sky, the air cooled. Lyons stared around him in disbelief.

"Ironman, we go," Thomas told him.

Gathering his equipment and weapons, following Thomas down the Indian trails, Lyons moved in a dream state, his mind not yet awake. Fragments of afternoon light blazed in deep shadows, polishing leaves with sharp brightness. Exotic butterflies fluttered in the rain forest's tangled growth, their wings in shadow, then suddenly flashing like neon, then lost again in the triple-canopy darkness. Lyons walked through the perfume of flowers and the stink of jungle slime. Ahead of them, he saw the line of warriors.

Another smell drifted to him, the foul stench of decomposition. In a few more steps, he saw the terrible source.

The Indian men pulled bodies of men and women and children from the dead brush. Around the clearing, every plant and tree had withered, yellowed. Yellow leaves carpeted the earth. The sunlight came unfiltered through the stick-bare branches of dead trees.

"Chlorine gas," Gadgets told him. "Point man found them a minute ago. We've counted fifteen people so far. We found a cook-fire, a few pots and pans, one old shotgun. I guess the slavers spotted them."

Steeling his gut, Lyons glanced at the bodies. Chlorine had seared the eyes and mouths of the Indians, had attacked their lungs. They had died screaming, their faces contorted, their mouths wide, caked with horrible wastes. Death-agony twisted their limbs. Now, after days of heat and humidity, the gases of decomposition ballooned their bodies, stretching taut the chlorine-seared skin.

"What are your men doing?" Lyons asked Thomas.

"We bury families."

Lyons shook his head. "No time."

"Then we burn—"

"Can't risk the smoke. The slavers are looking for us now, no doubt about it."

"Evil to leave the people for animals and birds.

"The longer the slavers live, the more people they gas, the more Indians they take for slaves. If we stay to bury these dead, more people die. That, surely, is the greater evil. I'm sorry. Please explain to the men. We must continue."

Thomas went to the men and told them what Lyons had said. To a man they protested, waving fists toward Lyons. But after another minute of talking, Thomas persuaded the men to leave the dead. One of the Xavantes pulled a feathered amulet from his neck and dropped it on the bodies. The line of men left the scene of mass murder.

Jogging forward, Lyons paused beside Lieutenant Silveres. "You saw that back there? We're after the scum who gassed those people. And we're going to waste them. I don't care if they're in Bolivia, or Brazil, or France. So if we have to cross your sacred national boundary, don't give me any crap."

"The defense of Brazil is the responsibility of the Brazilian army. We don't need meddling foreigners to protect our people."

"Don't need our help? Then why didn't *you* protect those people?"

Without giving the proud young officer time to reply, Lyons ran forward and took his place behind the point man.

16

As punishment for gas-bombing the gunboat, Chan Sann crucified the pilot. He did not listen to the French pilot's explanations about Williams's reported coordinates. He did not allow the pilot the mercy of suicide.

The French mercenary hung on a cross of planks, spikes driven through his forearms and feet. Flies and carrion beetles feasted on the raw flesh of his wounds. From time to time, the man returned to consciousness as the insects attacked his eyes. Incoherent with shock and agony and sunstroke, the dying pilot thrashed his head to shake away the insects, crying out in French and English. Sometimes he raved in Latin, intoning Catholic prayers, snatches of old hymns. As the sun sank, his motions slowed. They became spasmodic as blood and strength drained from him. Before he died, the beetles would eat his eyes.

Chan Sann sat in the shade of a rubber tree and watched the pilot suffer. Other Cambodians crowded around him, taking cold bottles of Brazilian beer from an ice chest. They chattered in their language, talking of the war against the bourgeoisie during the rule of their Communist master, Pol Pot. They had killed—with torture, Kalashnikov slugs, shovels, or starvation—all opposition to their regime. The opposition included doctors, lawyers, teachers, civil clerks, businessmen, shop owners, farmers, mechanics, laborers, Catholics, Buddhists, soldiers, officers. All educated Cambodians had died. All Cambodians who could read had died. All Cambodians who would not murder their neighbors, parents or children had died. Any failure to demonstrate unquestioning joy in the creation of the perfect Marxist state meant death.

During the three-year rule of Pol Pot, three and a half million of the counterrevolutionaries died, one-half of the population of Cambodia.

Now the Communist exiles joked of the extermination, describing tortures and mutilations that had amused them. They placed bets on when the pilot would die. Chan Sann did not participate in their game. He watched the French pilot with calm disdain.

"Tay!" Chan Sann spoke suddenly.

"Yes, Commander!" One of the Cambodians sprang to attention.

"He is a weakling. He will die soon. We will make him suffer more. Your knife, here...." Chan Sann made a motion.

"Yes, Commander!"

Running across the clearing, the soldier unsheathed his knife and slipped the blade into the abdomen of the naked Frenchman. With the skill of practice and experience, he dragged the tip of the knife across. The pain brought consciousness to the prisoner. The gash yawned, spilling out intestines. Flies descended in a cloud. The Frenchman looked down at the horror inflicted on him. He shrieked and he wailed.

Chan Sann smiled.

A walkie-talkie interrupted their game. Stopping his soldiers' giggles and chatter with a wave, Chan Sann pressed the radio's transmit key. "This is Chan Sann. Why do you disturb me?"

A voice blared. "Colonel Gomez has captured a river boat of workers. Wei Ho wants them for labor."

"Ready the helicopter."

As the forest shadows became enfolding darkness, the warriors neared the river. They had left behind the hills and ridges two hours before. The trail wove through swamplands and hardwood groves. Lyons drove Gadgets and Blancanales to the limits of their endurance. Even the Indian warriors moved slowly in the heat and humidity. Swarms of insects followed the line of men.

"Lyons!" Gadgets gasped, stumbling under his heavy backpack of electronics. "Where the hell are we racing to?"

"The river."

"It's less than an hour until sundown," Blancanales reminded him. "If we don't make camp, we'll have to put out lookouts and sentries in the dark."

"We'll camp at the river. Keep moving."

Using the forced march as a training exercise, Able Team had issued the new hand radios to Thomas and several Indians. Spreading out ahead of the main group, the Indians scouted parallel trails, looking for the easiest path, always watching for signs of slaver patrols. After the novelty of the "far-speaking boxes" wore off, the point men provided both security and speed. Marshes or dead ends never forced the heavily loaded main group to double back. Lyons rotated the point men, giving all the Indian warriors the opportunity to experiment with the twentieth-century devices.

Thomas received a radio message and translated it for Lyons, "One man smells the river."

"Great, pass the word along. We rest at the river." Lyons called back to Gadgets and Blancanales. "Ten or twenty more minutes."

"Joy to the world!" Gadgets gasped.

Another radio report came in. Thomas listened, then told Lyons, "There is fighting. He hears machine guns."

"How far?"

Thomas keyed his new hand radio to question the scout.

"He thinks it might be on the river."

"Tell him to keep going until he can see who's shooting at who."

Another scout buzzed Thomas. He listened for a moment. "It is steamer boat on the river. They fight with the army."

"With the army? Brazilian army or what?"

Thomas shrugged. "We go see."

An aerial sound cut off their talk. The line of men stared up at the dark branches above them. The distant rotor-whap of a helicopter came to them, then faded away. The warriors double-timed for the river.

Calling Lieutenant Silveres forward, Lyons briefed him as they followed Thomas. Despite his heavy pack, Lyons moved fast, striding up rises, jogging down. Breathless and sweat drenched, the young officer stumbled under his load of weapons and ammunition. But he never asked for rest.

"The river's a few minutes ahead," Lyons told him. "The point men have it in sight. They told us there's a steamer boat fighting with the army. They don't know who's on the steamer. They don't know what army it is. But we know who's in the helicopter. If it's your people up against the slavers, they might need help mucho pronto. So be prepared to introduce us. And do us a big favor, will you? Say something good. I mean, lay off about the CIA and gringos and the invasion of Brazil. Please? ¿Por favor?"

"I will tell—" the lieutenant gasped out words as he struggled to keep up with Lyons "—my superiors... what I have seen. You have... risked your lives... to help these Indians. I respect that. You rescued me from the foreigners. You fought the foreigners.... But the

Mamoré marks the boundary of Brazil. Only the army of Brazil. . .will fight in Brazil. It is not my decision or the decision of my superiors. It is the law. Because you come from a rich. . .military power. . .does not give you the right to fight in other countries. We are not cowards like the Europeans. The army of Brazil. . .and not the United States Army. . .defends our people.''

"Hey, kid, that's reasonable. But understand, we're Colonel John Phoenix's men from the United States of America and we're wiping out slave-takers. If you can help us do it, great. But to me, that river's only water.''

"Armed foreigners entering Brazil become the enemies of Brazil. When you cross the Mamoré, you become my enemy. I will do my duty.''

They heard the fire of automatic weapons. Lyons halted the line. A scout ran to Thomas. Thomas translated the report to Lyons and Lieutenant Silveres, "It is ended. The army take steamboat, take many farmers. We can do nothing.''

"What army? You mean slavers? Could your man see what's going on?''

Thomas looked Lieutenant Silveres straight in the face, sneered. "I mean Brazilian army take steamboat. You go see what goes on. It happens now.''

Advancing another hundred yards they came to a steep riverbank. Eroded by the flood current in the rainy season, a sheer dropoff overlooked a beach ten feet below and the river beyond. The line of men fanned out and crawled to the edge of the drop.

Several hundred yards downriver, Lyons saw a rust-streaked paddle-wheel boat aground on a curve in the river, the prow jammed into a sandbar. The amber light of dusk glowed on its white cabins and railings.

His binoculars closed the distance. A Huey helicopter bobbed on pontoons. An Oriental soldier threw a line from the Huey's side door to a Brazilian soldier on the rear deck of the steamer. The Brazilian caught the rope to secure the helicopter. Other lines held three olive drab PT boats to the aging river steamer. Stenciled unit numbers marked the sides of the patrol craft. Soldiers with unit patches and helmets swarmed over the decks of the steamer.

Panning up the length of the boat, Lyons knew why Thomas had sneered at the lieutenant. Through the binoculars, Lyons watched a scene of terror and murder. Soldiers pursued young girls on the decks of the paddle-wheel boat. Men and women struggled with the well-armed soldiers and took rifle butts in their faces. He saw a man with a shovel try to defend his wife; a soldier raised his auto-rifle: the muzzle flashed; an instant later, the sound of the burst drifted upriver. Soldiers dumped the body of the man into the river, tore at the clothing of the woman. Lyons watched her flail and scream, but her voice did not carry over the distance. A man and a woman jumped from the lowest deck, splashed through the waist-deep shallows. They didn't make the beach. Soldiers fired bursts into the water ahead of the couple, forced them to return. The soldiers clubbed the man and woman to the deck, kicked them. From time to time, other auto-bursts popped.

"There's the army of Brazil defending the people." Lyons passed the binoculars to the lieutenant. For a minute, Lieutenant Silveres watched. His hands shook. Without a word, avoiding Lyons's eyes, he returned the binoculars. He staggered back from the riverbank. Lyons heard him cursing.

Blancanales went to him. The older soldier stood with the lieutenant, gripped his shoulder. Lyons heard talk in Spanish and English, then a monologue of what had to

be obscenities in Portuguese. The young officer was rav-
ing, gesturing wildly, gesticulating toward the distant
river steamer. He clutched at the sling of his G-3. Blancanales had to restrain him, shove him back.

Lyons rushed to the side of his friend. "What's his
problem now?"

"There's an officer there. A Colonel Gomez. Appar-
ently Gomez was the one who sent Silveres out here. The
lieutenant is out here from the capital investigating a
rumor for the Bureau of Indians that all the Indians in
the region are gone. So Gomez sends the lieutenant and
his three men up here, and what happens? The slavers
take them, torture him to find out what the army and
the government told him about the problem out here.
The lieutenant's from an army family—very proud of
its history and its tradition of honor, patriotism—and
this is an insult to everything that he is."

"And Gomez is the one he radioed," Lyons de-
spaired. "So that bastard knows the score on Able
Team. Great. Just great. Your punk lieutenant's so
dumb arrogant he broadcasts the fact that there are only
three Americans and a platoon of Indians out here.
Great."

The lieutenant turned to him. "I apologize. You are
right, I.... But I did *not* send a radio message. I do not
know radios. I could not find the proper frequency. I
have not compromised your mission."

"Gomez is in charge of this region?" Lyons asked,
planning the next move. He glanced at the helicopter
and the several boats. "Once we're past him, there are
no more Brazilian units between us and the slaver
camps?"

The lieutenant nodded.

"We wipe out the colonel and his soldiers. We take
the boats, make it to the slavers. If you want to help

those people on that boat, Lieutenant, then we must cross the Mamoré. If we run into any loyal Brazilian army units, you will have to explain the situation. Law or patriotism or whatever.''

"There will be no problems whatsoever, my friends.'' The lieutenant stared across the Mamoré to Brazil. "In the name of the warrior you speak of, your Colonel Phoenix, that river is only water.''

Moving silently through the last minutes of dusk, they marched to the curve of the forest that jutted into the Mamoré. A few yards from the riverbank, Able Team and its Indian allies dropped their backpacks and prepared their weapons. Only a hundred yards of beach and shallow water separated them from the paddlewheeler. They heard the cries of women.

Gadgets monitored the slaver frequencies. "Ironman, Politician. Thomas. Speed it up. They just radioed the slaver base. They're going to pull the old boat off the sandbar and take the people to the camps.''

By touch, Blancanales passed a tube of face-blacking to Lieutenant Silveres. The Brazilian took a dab, then passed the blacking on to Thomas. All of the men shared it, ritually passing the blacking on to every man in the group, even those who already wore genipap. Hands checked magazines and bandoliers in the darkness.

Lyons conferred with the others. "I say we try to take the patrol boats and the helicopter first. If we can take a radio operator alive, without an alarm going out, we got a chance to cruise straight into their camp—as if we're bringing in the boatload of slaves. Thomas?''

"Maybe.''

"Lieutenant Silveres?''

"Very good.''

Blancanales agreed. "Sounds good to me. If everything goes perfectly...."

"Yeah, yeah. We do it, okay? Gadgets, you stay here and listen for any Mayday calls...."

"Forget that. You'll need me. I'll set up the recorder."

"Good enough. Thomas, tell your men. We take the boats and helicopter with knives and machetes. When we have the radios, we take the riverboat."

Like shadows within shadows, the warriors slipped through the last tangles of the rain forest and snaked down the embankment. Finally they saw the riverboat close up. What they saw stopped them.

17

Like party lights, strings of electric bulbs blazed along the rails of the old paddle-wheel steamer. The glaring points of incandescence blitzed the darkness, making the night day around the helicopter, the patrol boats, and the paddle-wheeler itself.

On the aft cargo deck, the uniformed soldiers of Colonel Gomez secured lines to the patrol boats as they prepared to tow the steamboat into deeper water. On the prow, Asian sentries in shapeless unmarked olive drab fatigues paced the brightly lit passenger decks.

One hundred fifty feet from the paddle-wheel steamer, Able Team watched. They sprawled in the tangled reeds of the riverbank. The lights were also illuminating the shallows, the beach, the trees of the forest.

"That kills it," Gadgets hissed.

"No, it doesn't," Lyons snapped back. "We angle in from the front. If we keep the riverboat between us and the other boats, we can use the Berettas to take out those forward sentries."

"I don't trust the Berettas to do it," Blancanales whispered to Gadgets and Lyons. The three men crowded shoulder to shoulder. Lieutenant Silveres listened from the other side of Blancanales. "Even if we hit both of them, make instant kills, they'll fall on the deck.. .."

"Yeah," Lyons agreed. "And anybody could be behind them, see it happen. Listen, I can do a hundred feet underwater, that'll get me within—"

"That'll get you dead, hotshot," Gadgets told him.

"Nah. Watch them," Lyons argued. "Sometimes for thirty seconds or a minute or two minutes, they've got their backs turned. Or they're off the deck. I chance it, I move fast. . . ."

"Hey, Hardman One, wise up," insisted Gadgets. "Just 'cause you're brave don't mean you won't die. If you come up short, if they see you, they got you. We can't chance it, not even to help those farmers. Besides, you'd be down there with the crocodiles, and you're wearing your lizard-attracting lotion."

"I do it," Lieutenant Silveres told them.

Blancanales shook his head. The lieutenant continued.

"Listen to me, Yankee. If they see me, they will see this uniform. They will think I'm with that traitor, Gomez."

The warm river water closed around him. Slowly, silently, Lieutenant Silveres slipped through the reeds and the marsh grasses, his hands clawing into the slime. He pressed his belly into the mud, bending his back to keep his face above the surface. As the muddy water deepened, Silveres moved faster, digging his boots into the bottom, pushing through the shallows.

A hundred lights streaked the river. Reflected from the gently waving surface, the rusted paddle steamer became a shimmering white dream ship resplendent with electric jewels.

Silveres watched the sentries crossing and recrossing the decks. Staying in the darkness and mud of the shallows, he watched for a chance to swim to the steamer. The sentries carried their automatic rifles loose in their hands, ready to fire, ready to end his life.

A few minutes before, the talk of death had not

seemed real. He had volunteered with full consideration of the risk. But he was thinking then of death in the abstract, as only a word.

Now he thought of the other night when the Cuban put the pistol to his head. But death had been an abstraction that night also. After the mercenaries had ambushed his men, killing two, capturing him and the seventeen-year-old private, the lieutenant had not felt fear. Shock numbed him. He endured the beating and torture because he did not believe the scene real. His mind did not accept the reality, therefore he escaped the very worst of the pain. When the Cuban put the pistol to the head of Guerimo, the teenager who hoped to own a long-distance truck, who wrote love letters to five girls by hand-copying one letter five times, only then had the lieutenant snapped from his trance. He tried to reason with the Cuban. The flash of the pistol seemed a crime beyond belief. Tradition and pride did not allow him to beg for his own life. He thought of nothing, waited for the nightmare to end at the end of the pistol pointed at his head.

Watching from outside the Indian camp, the gringos and the Chicanos who rescued him believed him brave, fearless. But they did not know the truth.

Now, lying in the warm slime, he felt fear. It coiled inside him, writhed in his bowels. His body waited for his mind to command action, but he did not move. He watched the Asian mercenaries pace the deck.

A woman sobbed. From one of the cabins, the cry rose and fell. She shrieked, pleaded. Then silence came abruptly. Then laughter burst out.

Lieutenant Silveres knew he had more than bullets and a quick death to fear. Perhaps they would capture him again. No, not again. He could not, he would not be captured again. He could not hide within his shock again. He would die first.

Brave words. He lay in the marshy shallows of the Mamoré because of his brave words to the gringos. But he did not move. Fear whipped within him as his imagination gave him images. Death by bullets. Death by knives. Death by pliers to his genitals.

Fear stopped his breathing. He forced his lungs to suck air, forced his chest to expel the air. His body was immobilized with fear. He concentrated only on breathing.

Several Asians stepped from the paddle-wheeler to the helicopter tethered to the side. The blades spun, a whine rising as the engine warmed, the blades becoming a blur. Water sprayed in all directions.

Now! Now the sentries would not see him. He touched the flap securing the Italian pistol. Would it fire after minutes under water? He checked the flap of the thigh pocket carrying the hand radio. Would he lose it as he swam? Would the plastic protect it from the river's water? No time for more thoughts, no time for more fear. Silveres kicked against the mud, stroked desperately through the muddy water. He took a last look at the rotting ship's decks. The helicopter's rotor storm sprayed muddy water everywhere.

He sucked down a last breath and went under the water, swimming with all his strength, scissoring his legs again and again, trying to gain every possible yard before his lungs forced him to the surface.

A pain seared his leg. Another hit his ribs. So this is how bullets feel, he thought. But he didn't stop. Perhaps he could live if he reached the hull of the steamer, perhaps he could kill the mercenary before the mercenary killed him. The lieutenant feared death like never before. Fear made him strong and fast. Fear of death made the pain in his lungs nothing.

The Cambodian watched the helicopter of Commander Chan Sann soar away. Spray drifted in the air for seconds, misting around the bulbs on the upper rails. Water covered everything. The Cambodian resumed his circuit of the lowest deck, wiping the river water from his automatic rifle.

He did not like the rifle. A Heckler & Koch, it weighed more than a Kalashnikov. The recoil jarred his slight body. The incomprehensible mechanics of the bolt confused him. He wished he could carry a Kalashnikov.

The woman his friends had in the cabin screamed again. He stopped at the port of the cabin and peered in through the louvers.

Some of his friends held her while each in turn took her. Soon his turn would come. He thought of the years after the Victory of the Proletariat in his province. He'd had all the village girls. It had been good to be a soldier then. Chan Sann said the Chinese Wei Ho talked of a World Victory of the Proletariat. The Cambodian smiled. Then he would have all the girls of the world.

A hand grasped the railing. The Cambodian started away from the louvers to gaze at the hand. It was wet with water and blood. He heard gasping. Something fluttered against the hull. He snapped off the safety of his G-3. He advanced as one of the Brazilians dragged himself up and over the railing.

Water and blood flowing from his uniform, the Brazilian slapped at his body. A silver thing flashed and twisted in the glare from the lights. The Brazilian hit at the thing again and again with his hand.

Piranha! The Cambodian lowered his rifle and stared

at the fish flopping on the deck. He studied the mouth of the piranha. He saw bloody, needle-sharp teeth. He had never seen one alive. What a beautiful creature!

Lieutenant Silveres ignored the pain from the last piranha still clamped to his back. The predator was twisting and shaking, trying to rip away a mouthful of flesh and cloth. He saw the Asian sentry smiling at the piranha dying on the deck. Glancing fore and aft on the walkway, he did not see any other sentry.

Praying the pistol would fire, the lieutenant slipped it out of its holster and thumbed back the hammer. With no more sound than a fist against flesh, the slug punched through the Asian's skull. The dead man fell to the deck. The bullet bounced off the warped planks of the deck, clattered against the cabins.

A man laughed. Watching the single lighted cabin on the deck, Silveres gripped the pistol, then reached behind him to jerk the last piranha from his flesh. Warm and slick with his blood, the fish wriggled from his hand. It flopped on the deck. Silveres crushed it with his boot. He grabbed the sentry's corpse by one arm and dragged it from the walkway. The man's G-3 scraped on the planks.

Footsteps crossed the deck above him. Pushing the corpse under a bench, the lieutenant took the G-3, reset the safety and slung the rifle over his shoulder. He held the pistol against his leg as he hurried to the prow. He did not see a second sentry. A woman's scream came from the lighted cabin. He heard the sound of a head hammered against wood. He looked back. Could he help the woman?

The cabin door opened. Silveres pressed himself flat in a doorway. An Asian mercenary laughed as he stepped out of the cabin. He waved to other men laughing inside. A beer bottle flew out, bounced past the rail and into the river. The second sentry closed the door, laughing, and walked toward the prow.

The sentry saw the blood and the dead fish. He stooped over, touched the blood. Watching from the doorway, Silveres saw the man scan the planks. The trail of blood led to the bench concealing the dead sentry. The Asian was following the blood across the deck.

Silveres stepped from the doorway and strode directly toward the Asian. He felt the fear in his gut again, cold and writhing. Would the mercenary see that he was a stranger? Would the mercenary call out the others?

The Asian smiled to the Brazilian officer approaching him. Silveres kept his face expressionless, his stride regular despite the fear knotted in his chest. Then the cabin door opened again. He snapped up the pistol, fired point-blank into the Asian's face. The man fell back, the smile fixed, one eye a wound.

The lieutenant spun around as an Asian wearing no pants weaved out from the cabin and lurched to the railing. Holding on to the railing, he sent a stream of urine into the river.

A slug smashed through the back of his head.

Without thinking, without hesitation, the lieutenant burst into the cabin firing silent slugs. He killed two of the mercenaries before the others turned. One Asian grabbed for a rifle, took a bullet in the chest, a second in his face. Another drew back to throw a beer bottle, took two bullets in the chest. Silveres jerked the last man from the motionless, unconscious young woman on the bed. He jammed the pistol under the mercenary's chin and pulled the trigger.

A knife ripped his leg. The lieutenant pointed the pistol at the blood-frothed face of a man on the floor, sending a slug through his brain.

Dead rapists sprawled everywhere. Silveres aimed to

fire another bullet through the brain of the nearest man
but stopped. He did not have the ammunition to waste
on dead men. He pressed the magazine release on the
Beretta, counted the remaining cartridges. Three, plus
one in the chamber. He slapped the magazine back. He
took the knife from the last man he had killed. Silveres's
own blood glistened on the blade. If any of the mercenaries still lived, he would cut their throats.

He kicked all the dead men. He jabbed them with the
knife. None moved. Slipping the knife under his belt, he
checked the woman. She breathed jerkily. Blood flowed
from cuts on her face and the back of her head. He
threw a blanket over her battered naked body, then
eased out the cabin door.

Forcing his lungs to slow their gasping, the lieutenant
glanced fore and aft. No one. His heart hammered in his
ears. He staggered as he walked, steadying himself with
a hand on the railing. He continued around the prow to
where he could look down the other walkways.

Brazilian soldiers—traitors, worse than mercenaries
because they betrayed their uniform and their father-
land—worked at the back of the steamer, jumping from
the rear deck to the patrol boats. But no sentry paced
the deck.

Starting to the stairs to the upper decks, his knees
buckled. He staggered, held himself upright with the
banister. He sucked down several breaths, listened for
steps or voices above him. But the ringing in his ears
deafened him. He looked behind him.

Blood marked his every step on the deck. He looked
at his uniform. Glistening red covered the olive drab of
his pants. Blood flowed from the piranha wounds on his
side and back, mingled with the flows from the other
bites and the knife slash on his legs.

He sat on the stairs and looked to the dark riverbank

where the North Americans and Indians waited. He had
cleared the sentries from only one deck. He could do no
more. Slipping the plastic-protected hand radio from his
pants' thigh pocket, he wiped off the blood and water
and tore open the bag. He switched on the power, keyed
the transmit. "I am not a coward, but I cannot...
wounds and blood. Can you see.... Can...."

"Lieutenant!" A voice blared from the radio, like a
shout on the silent deck. Silveres stared at the radio in
his hand, found the volume dial, quieted the voice.
"Lieutenant. Are you wounded?"

"Yes. I have killed the mercenaries. The mercenaries
on the lowest deck. But I cannot... I cannot go to the
other decks."

"Your deck is clear? You see no one?"

"I killed them."

"We'll be there soonest."

As he watched, the Chicano he knew as the Politico
left the reeds, strode through the water, holding his
rifle/grenade launcher and radio out of the silt-brown
river. The lights on the riverboat illuminated him as if
he walked on the beach in midday. He crossed the shallows quickly and climbed over the rail. He waved to the
riverbank. A line of men followed, holding weapons
and radios above the water. One Indian man jerked
sideways, grabbed at something in the water. They ran
through the water, scrambled to the deck. The Indians
jerked piranha from two of their fellow tribesmen and
the gringo who wore the native body-blacking and loincloth. A second line of men hurried through the shallows.

Hands touched the lieutenant's wounds. The Politico
examined the bites and slashes. Men with blood streaming down their bodies passed the lieutenant, their feet
silent on the creaky old stairs.

Blancanales's hand radio buzzed. "Politician here."

"This is the Wizard. All clear on this side. I count eight dead gooks so far."

"How's the soldier?" Lyons said, his silenced Beretta in one hand, his radio in the other.

"No problem. He'll have a few scars."

"Is a war like this?" Lieutenant Silveres asked the two North American commandos.

The American he knew as Ironman laughed out loud. "What do you think this is?"

18

Their wet sandals silent on the warped, rotting decking, Lyons and three Xavante warriors slipped past the dark cabins of the first deck. Dripping river water and blood, their blackened bodies glistened in the railings' brilliant lights. Blood flowed from two piranha bites on Lyons, a deep snip from the flesh of his thigh and twin semicircles of teeth punctures on his left elbow. Other men bled also, their blood spattering the walkway.

Crouch-walking beneath louvered ports, listening for voices or movement inside without pausing, they crept toward the cargo deck. Lyons stopped at the open door to a lighted cabin, took a look inside.

Clothes, shoes, books littered bunk beds. An Asian mercenary sat on a lower tunk, tearing open cardboard boxes, searching through the possessions of a family. Lyons chanced another look into the cabin. He saw no one on the bunk bed against the opposite wall. Gripping his Beretta with both hands, he stepped into the doorway. He sighted through the bunk's steel frame to the mercenary's head. He put the bullet in the Asian's right temple. The body fell sideways on the bed, as if the man slept.

Continuing, they came to stairs. Shouts and cries came from the deck above them. Feet scrambled somewhere, the woodwork of the old steamer creaking. Lyons pointed to a Xavante, pointed to a shadow. He touched his eye, then indicated the flight of stairs. The Xavante nodded, stood in the shadow. Invisible, he guarded the stairs, his black-bladed machete in his hand.

Lyons watched the Brazilian soldier on the first patrol boat. He called to the cargo deck. A voice answered. Boots crossed the deck.

A patrol boat's motor rumbled. Behind the windshield on the open bridge, a soldier cranked a steering wheel, then called out. A soldier stepped over the paddle-wheeler's rail, carefully extended one leg to the gunwale of the patrol boat, shifted his weight to step across the gap.

Whipping up the Beretta, Lyons sighted with both hands. He waited an instant. At the moment the soldier transferred his weight to his forward leg, a 9mm subsonic slug shattered the knee. The soldier fell into the river, screaming for help.

Brazilian soldiers crowded the railing. A man ran to the rail with a rope, threw one end to the man thrashing in the water. Lyons dashed to the end of the walkway. He looked around the corner, saw no other soldiers on the cargo deck, squinted past the blazing lights on the rail, saw soldiers at the helms of the second and third patrol boats.

Taking five silent strides across the deck, Lyons raised the Beretta. He jammed the titanium suppressor against the head of the first soldier, sent a slug through his skull. The men leaning against the railing turned at the sudden movement, saw a black-painted six-foot-one wild man. The Beretta snapped three-shot bursts into their chests and faces. The fourth soldier grabbed at the G-3 slung over his shoulder. A Xavante stepped past Lyons and swung his machete with both hands. The severed head fell into the river.

A three-shot burst through the head dropped the nearest helmsman. Lyons stepped over corpses, sighted on the chest of a soldier on the second patrol boat. The soldier raised an auto-rifle. Lyons slipped in blood, sent a burst through the boat's windshield.

Waving the muzzle of the G-3 at Lyons's chest, the soldier pulled the trigger. Nothing. He jerked back the cocking lever even as three 9mm steel-cored slugs tore through his heart. A dead man's auto-fire slammed into the deck and gunwale of the patrol boat as the man fell.

On the third boat, the helmsman took cover. Passing a stack of head-high wooden crates, Lyons heard the scuff of boots. A dying soldier fell at his feet, the back of his head spraying blood. He saw a Xavante dodge through the cargo, his bloody machete held high.

Auto-fire slammed into the crates. Lyons fell back, scrambling for cover. High-velocity .308 NATO slugs splintered wood, smashed through five-gallon cans of motor oil. Holstering his Beretta, Lyons slipped the Atchisson from his back and pulled back the actuator to strip the first round from the magazine.

Firing broke out on the upper decks. A Brazilian soldier flew backward over the third deck railing, crashing down on the crates, tumbling to the deck in front of Lyons. Alive, but badly wounded and disoriented, the man struggled to his feet. Lyons shoved him into the open. Auto-fire from the patrol boat spun the Brazilian.

Sighting on the muzzle-flash, Lyons fired three blasts. The 1200-feet-per-second steel balls disintegrated the fiberglass and plywood of the patrol craft's gunwale. Lyons crouch-walked to another row of stacked boxes and fifty-gallon drums and checked out the deck of the craft.

In the glare of the aft rail's electric lights, he saw a battered and impact-pocked G-3, a hand caught by a finger in the trigger guard. The rifleman thrashed ten feet away, his eyes and forehead gone, his right forearm gone, a hideous cry choking from his throat. Lyons raised the Atchisson to fire a mercy blast into the man's brain but did not.

A Xavante with a Remington 870 crouched beside Lyons. Lyons hand-signaled for the warrior to cover him, then dashed to the rail and vaulted to the patrol boat. Holding the Atchisson at his hip, he stepped over the blinded and dying soldier, stole a glance inside the craft's small cabin, whipped his head back fast. A pistol shot flashed.

Stepping back three paces, Lyons put two blasts through the bulkhead, darted in as a wound-riddled Brazilian lurched toward him, a pistol rising. The Atchisson roared. The suddenly headless soldier bounced off a radio console, his one remaining shoulder and arm whipping about.

Lyons looked out the impromptu window in the craft's cabin. Through the shredded plywood and hanging wires, he scanned the second patrol boat. A Xavante searched the boat. On the prow, concealed behind a canvas-covered, pedestal-mounted M-60, an Asian waited in ambush with a pistol. Lyons sighted on the mercenary's head and blew it away. The Indian saw the headless corpse splash into the river. He looked up, his eyes searching the patrol boat for whoever had saved him.

"Xavante!" Lyons called out as he changed mags on the auto-shotgun. The Indian waved.

Feet thudded on the deck of the patrol boat. The wounded Brazilian's hideous crying was cut off with the sound of a machete chopping meat. A warrior peered cautiously into the cabin, smiled to Lyons, motioned him out.

"Shadowman!" Gadgets called out from the rail of the third deck. "Did we make it?"

Lyons glanced back to the craft's console. Steel double-ought and number two shot had smashed the metal and plastic and torn away a panel to expose circuitry. He stepped closer to check the power switch. Off. Lyons called back to his friend.

"No messages out."

"Yeeeaah! Victory party time!"

Coarse featured, their hands gnarled by decades of working in the fields, the grandfathers spoke for family clans. Their wide-shouldered sons and grandsons stood behind them. A barrel-bellied merchant spoke for another group of families. They argued and shouted, interrupting each other, some men leaning to within inches of Gadgets's face to make their statements, all shouting Portuguese. Gadgets understood nothing.

"They want to avenge themselves on Gomez and the soldiers who are alive," Lieutenant Silveres translated. A nurse, wife to one of the settlers, stitched the slashes in the young officer's legs. The lieutenant spoke to the group of elders. They turned their shouting to him.

Blancanales cleaned Lyons's piranha bites. He pulled back a flap of skin on Lyons's upper leg to spray the wound with alcohol. Lyons went rigid with pain. The alcohol dissolved the genipap, leaving a splotch of Southern California tan surrounding the gaping tear.

"Looks like the fish liked that lizard lotion, too," Gadgets joked to Lyons. Lyons ignored him, his eyes closed, his face set against the pain of the disinfectant. "But it could have been worse, you walking around in that water with only a jockstrap on...."

"Any of our men get hit?" Lyons gritted through clamped jaws.

"Hit by fish. But we took these slavers cold. No firefight here. We came in the side doors fast, caught them in a cross fire...."

Gadgets pointed to the wide doors on each side of the passenger lounge. "They had the passengers jammed in here, everyone down on the floor. Only the Gomez-men and the gooks standing up. Gomez saw his men dropping, saw us, went down on his knees begging. Mucho macho bad man."

Now the lounge served as a hospital. Wounded men lay on the floor, tended by their families. Women comforted women assaulted by the slavers. A knot of grim-faced men stared at a door guarded by Indian warriors. Inside, ropes lashed Gomez and two soldiers to chairs. Of all the slavers, only Gomez, one of his Brazilians and a Cambodian mercenary survived.

Pale with blood loss, the lieutenant slumped. The nurse braced him, kept him from falling to the floor. Blancanales finished with Lyons, then eased the lieutenant down. Blancanales and the nurses eased the crowd of shouting elders back.

"Civilians! They talk without end, I cannot argue more with them," the lieutenant sighed. "They want the traitors.... They will not listen to the law."

"First we interrogate the three of them," Lyons said, "then the settlers can have them."

"No!" The lieutenant bolted upright. "Gomez betrayed his country and his uniform. He will be judged and executed by the armed forces."

"He take our women!" A young man shouted in broken English. "He kill my cousin. His wife alone now. With five children. We hang the colonel, cut off his balls and hang him!"

"I say give him to the people," Lyons commented.

"No!" The lieutenant countered. "Military justice."

Blancanales's low, resonant voice interrupted the

shouting. "If the settlers want revenge, good. But it will not feed the children or help the women who lost their husbands. If they kill Gomez, they will only kill one slaver. They must still fear all the others out there."

"What others?" the young farmer demanded. "We see all dead."

"Gomez and the soldiers were only one patrol. There are many more soldiers in this region. Mercenaries. Killers. They take Indians to be slaves. They wanted you for slaves. Soon we go to attack them. If you want revenge, come. Then your families will be safe."

"More soldiers? Of Brazil?"

"No!" the lieutenant shouted. "Traitors. Mercenaries in the uniform of the army of Brazil," he explained in Portuguese.

Fear and hatred and rage pulsed in the faces of the men. Some of them rushed away to tell the others in the lounge. Women shrieked. All the men, even a few of the injured, crowded around Lieutenant Silveres and the foreigners, shouting, waving their fists.

"They want the rifles of the dead soldiers," the lieutenant translated. "To defend themselves. Some of them want to know where the other soldiers are. To attack them. Others want the army to come. Others fear the army, because of Gomez."

"Will you come with us?" Blancanales asked the crowd in Portuguese. "To attack the slavers?"

"Yes. We attack!"

Lyons grinned to Blancanales. "Okay, recruiter. Make a deal with these people."

In the next half hour, Blancanales and Lieutenant Silveres negotiated an agreement with the settlers. Balancing the blood lust of the men against the concern of their wives, Blancanales stated that he needed boat pilots and dependable men to fire heavy weapons, machine guns and grenade launchers, at a distance from the actual fighting. He would not risk the lives of the family men in close fighting.

As payment, and to help the families of men murdered on the riverboat, the settler community would receive all equipment captured from the slavers—boats, weapons, radios and whatever the settlers found at the camp, except for equipment stolen from the government of Brazil.

A work party with lights and power tools left immediately on one of the PT boats. They would strip the heavy weapons and their mounts from the several slaver cruisers and airboats on the other river. Able Team wanted the weapons to be mounted on the fast PT boats.

Other settlers smeared black paint on the riverboat's dinghies. The small aluminum boats and an aluminum canoe found in the cargo would take the assault force ashore. A blacksmith wired sheets of steel together to protect the men who would stay in the patrol boats, to machine-gun and bombard the camp from a distance.

Activity and war spirit replaced the settlers' grief as the refloated riverboat, its lights and windows blacked out, steamed downstream. At the fork where three rivers met—the one from Bolivia, the Mamoré and the river leading to the nuclear complex—the riverboat would go no farther.

Gadgets assembled his electronic gear in the mahogany-and-polished brass bridge of the old paddlewheeler. First, he swept out the shattered glass, then wiped the captain's blood from the walls and floor. The sixty-year-old white-haired immigrant from Zaire had died with a pistol in his hand, defending his ship and his passengers.

Switching on the recorder playback, Gadgets listened to the tape of slaver frequencies during the assault. While he worked, he heard static, the pops and squeaks of over-the-horizon transmitters disrupting the slaver radio frequencies, electronic noise from space. Then came the Asian voice, the words in textbook English, yet alien and macabre when Chan Sann spoke.

No. Gadgets shook away the thought. *That's superstition. It's not in his voice. It's what I've seen in the last three days. Now I can't hear that Cambodian talk without thinking about dead people.*

Chan Sann relayed a curt announcement of the capture of the steamboat to Abbott—an American, Gadgets judged from his Massachusetts accent. Other transmissions announced numbers of workers captured and the departure of Chan Sann by helicopter. But during the time of the assault, nothing. No clicking of a transmit key, no emergency call words, no voices cut off by rifle fire, nothing.

We did it. Took them out without a sound.

Spreading out his shortwave and scrambler on the captain's chart table, he carefully positioned the units. He set a note pad precisely where his right hand would rest. Then the tape antenna went up the flagpole.

Keying codes, receiving automatic coded replies, Gadgets taped a burst of Stony Man intelligence transmitted from Virginia, relayed by satellite. He replayed it through the scrambler as he wrote out his own message on the yellow pad.

His writing stopped. He listened another moment, then rushed out to find Lyons and Blancanales. Replaying the tape, they heard a conspiracy of depravity and assassination beginning before they were born.

Now, that conspiracy threatened every living man and woman and child in the Free World, and unknown generations of the unborn.

19

Born the eldest son of a Chinese warlord, Wei Ho enjoyed the vast wealth of his clan. The Wei clan had ruled Jiangsu province from the time of his great-grandfather, a puppet for the British invaders of China. After the English introduced opium and addiction to millions of Chinese, the Wei controlled the drug trade in their region. They reaped an unending harvest of gold. The family maintained an army of mercenaries to enslave the people of the province, enforcing their sovereignty through assassination and atrocity.

The first-born son knew only palaces, European tutors and luxury. After an education in the finest English prep schools and universities, Wei Ho traveled the capitals of Europe, tasting the life and vices of royalty and the very wealthy before returning to China to assume control of his clan's drug trade in Shanghai.

Modern, designed by Europeans wanting a city of boulevards and lights, Shanghai represented a door to the hundreds of millions of the Chinese nation. There, English and French and Portuguese exacted the wealth of the vast but weak nation through "concessions" imposed by military threat. The European masters erected ornate offices and regal homes, built opera houses and theaters for their own entertainment. Chinese police excluded Chinese from the European sections where the foreigners promenaded on jacaranda-shaded boulevards in the finest Paris fashions.

As China entered the twentieth century, the adventurous and radical among the nation's youth sought the freedom and the Western ideas of Shanghai. Actors, writers, poets crowded the ghettoes. Young girls sought careers denied by their traditions. Idealists read Marx and Engels and Lenin, dreamed of a workers' paradise in China.

This became Wei Ho's world. His playboy life-style and underworld connections endeared him to the decadent rich. The artists enjoyed his patronage. The beautiful young men and women enjoyed his exotic drugs—the finest opium, cocaine from far-off Bolivia, red hashish from Beirut, kif from North Africa. The radicals appreciated his education in philosophy, endlessly discussing their plans of political and cultural revolution in cafés and bookstores as Wei Ho, in his tailored English suits, smoking English cigarettes, smiled at their fantasies.

One night, not in a bookstore or coffee shop or lecture hall, he saw Lan Pin. The girl who would later rule the destinies of a billion Chinese ran from the stage of a cabaret theater, sequins in her bobbed and curled hair, sweat streaking her makeup. When the young Chinese playboy, dressed like a European prince, caught up with her and simply smiled to her, the actress invited him back to her tiny dressing room. They chatted of art and beauty, she thanked him for his roses and champagne. The cabaret's owner interrupted. The fat old man with a blind eye took the beautiful young Lan Pin away to his apartment.

Wei Ho felt no jealousy. He knew of the young girl's relationship with the old man. He knew every detail of her flighty career. Riding in limousines to the nightclubs where Chinese youth affected the fads of Europe and America, dancing to jazz and drinking gin, Lan Pin presented herself as an actress. But she played her best roles in the beds of theater promoters and playwrights, musical directors and matinee idols. Her favors won her small roles in minor productions, but never the notice of the critics, nor the adoration of the audience, never stardom. Wei Ho courted her to offer a different sort of stardom, in roles where the ambitious, amoral young girl would excel.

He soon took her to the Persian splendor of his apartment and introduced her to opium. Sprawled on the soft carpets, she traveled the fantasy worlds of his drugs. She listened to his tight dictatorial voice attempt whispers. She felt his cold hands undress her. He offered her pleasure and wealth if she accepted a role...to become his mistress.

Lan Pin accepted instantly. As his lover, she knew she would enjoy the best circles of Shanghai society. She would enjoy his wealth.

Wei Ho demanded total subservience. He took her as mistress and student, training her in conversation, the social arts, how to subtly manipulate. He hired aging courtesans to instruct the girl in the erotic arts.

She had misunderstood the role he offered. When she finally had the talents of a high-priced prostitute, he dispatched her to his father.

In the old man's bed, she spied for Wei Ho. Learning of an important conference of warlords, Wei Ho arranged his father's assassination, and the taking of his empire.

Wei Ho rose to dominate the drug gangs of pre-Revolutionary China through the use of assassins and young girls. Wei Ho rewarded his star spy with a feature role in a film production. Lan Pin finally gained the wealth and stardom she desired.

Soon she desired more, much more. She had seen her

mentor's rise to power. Exploiting her sudden fame when her movie became a box-office smash, she sought introductions to politicians, outspoken army officers, Communist Party leaders.

Wei Ho felt no jealousy. Famine and war stalked China in the 1930s. He knew the value of a woman in government.

As an actress in cabarets and theaters, she knew the thrill of an audience. She loved the sensation of standing on a stage before hundreds of adoring watchers. But the small audiences of theaters no longer satisfied her. She dreamed of greater adoration. One warm night, after miles in a car crowded with Communist leaders, she followed her friends upstairs, found herself looking out over a sea of faces, thousands upon thousands into the distance.

After that night, she lusted for power—the greater power of life or death over the common people, the masses. Wei Ho guided her. He selected her lovers.

Lan Pin's intellectual lovers taught her the rhetoric of revolution. Her wealthy patrons talked of capitalism. The young men of the Communist Party talked of a People's War.

She watched Mao Tse-Tung gathering support. She saw him as the emerging leader of an overwhelming popular movement. Though he had already married a peasant girl, the beautiful actress, perfumed and demure in her silk gowns, speaking the approved Marxist clichés, recognized no bourgeois vows. She flattered and charmed the revolutionary, parroting his dogma, marveling at the beauty and philosophy of his poetry. Finally, the awkward young idealist succumbed to her charms.

She drove away Mao's pregnant wife, and she married him. She abandoned her stage name of Lan Pin, took the name Jiang Qing. She told Mao her change of names symbolized her change from frivolous actress to a cadre worker devoted to the Revolution. The change in names also severed her links with her many other lovers. Through Mao Tse-Tung, Jiang Qing would later dictate every detail of Communist life in a mad drive for total power through continuous revolution—staging operas, writing billboards, appointing generals, executing teachers, destroying universities. The promoters and agents who had exploited the vulnerable young Lan Pin received death sentences signed by a mysterious Jiang Qing.

Wei Ho remained her friend and confidant throughout her rise to power in the next decades. The two of them supplied drugs and prostitutes—young girls and boys—to the leaders of the proletariat. They gathered information on forbidden pleasures. In the times of starvation and hardship, they smuggled European delicacies and luxuries to those who could pay—the People's Army generals and the Communist Party cadres.

Compiling a history of secret crimes against the People, the two conspirators blackmailed concessions from the Party leadership. They threatened the ideologues with the ax of the truth. Wei Ho and Jiang Qing created a clique of power within the Communist Party.

In the 1960s, Mao Tse-Tung lost day-to-day control of the Party to his wife and her clique. Jiang Qing screened the chairman's visitors, denying appointments to whomever displeased her. She rewrote her husband's political statements. She appointed commissars and provincial officials. In a secret coup d'état, her Gang of Four seized China.

As the mentor of the empress of the People's Repub-

lic of China, Wei Ho ruled a billion Chinese. Yet he
knew his power to be fragile. Enemies surrounded
China: the Soviet Union to the north, India to the west,
the United States to the east. And within China, two
decades of suffering and unending labor had sapped the
revolutionary spirit of the people. Impatient with the
promises of a future Marxist utopia, they wanted the
benefits of the revolution immediately. Village councils
defied the Central Committee, reinstituted bourgeois
crimes such as private gardens, neighborhood vegetable
markets, tradesmen shops and vendors. Worker com-
mittees wanted better workers to receive more pay.
These small occurrences of individual enterprise
presented greater threats to the Dictatorship of the Proletariat than any foreign army.

The Gang of Four declared the Cultural Revolution,
marshaling the forces of the nation's delinquent and
discontented youth. Mobs destroyed every vestige of the
counterrevolution, burning universities, beating teachers to death, hanging merchants, dragging the critics of
the Party leadership through the streets until only bones
and ragged meat remained. Chaos and murder swept
China for years.

But Wei Ho and the Gang of Four could not chal-
lenge their foreign enemies with mobs. The Peoples'
Army, equipped with captured Japanese weapons and
castoff Russian rifles, posed no threat to any modern
army. Though the physicists of China had designed and
assembled an atomic bomb, China lacked the aircraft or
missiles to strike a target. The regime remained vulnerable to any world power willing to mount an invasion.

Local conflict in Vietnam provided the inspiration for
development and use of weapons for global conflict.
Wei Ho studied the war of attrition waged between the
United States and the Communists. He read the reports

of action, defeats, atrocities published in America and Europe. He watched tapes of television specials condemning the American efforts to defend the Republic of South Vietnam. Nowhere did the media mention the Communist methods of control over the people. He saw photos of children killed by American air strikes, but not of village chiefs impaled on poles, no photos of village defenders' children disemboweled and beheaded, no photos of young girls with their lips cut away for smiling at American soldiers. Wei Ho discovered the peculiar Western neurosis of self-flagellation and self-deception. Americans and Europeans denied the fact of Communist atrocities, and if confronted with proof in color backed with sworn witnesses, actually believed themselves guilty for Communist murders and mutilations. This neurosis became the central concept of the conspiracy he outlined to the Gang of Four.

Communism could not hope to gain world dominance through economic force, he explained. All Communist states went bankrupt shortly after their revolutions. Slave labor by millions of political prisoners succeeded in maintaining a facade of progress, but executions and mass death soon depleted the legions of slaves. China and Vietnam had followed Stalin's methods of economic advancement and met with the same inevitable collapse.

But terror promised easy victory over the bourgeois democracies of the West. Europeans and Americans lacked the will to endure the slightest inconvenience. If an elected president or prime minister failed to maintain an ever-rising standard of living, the voters found another face and voice to speak from their televisions. If a war conflicted with the hedonism of the youth, millions marched on the capitals, demanding an end to their nations' involvement, regardless of the consequences. How would these same citizens respond to a war without frontiers? A war threatening every citizen with death at any moment? How many casualties would they suffer before they demanded peace at any price? Before they accepted any government? Any regime?

The weapons of this war would be compact atomic bombs. If small enough to be concealed in an automobile, Chinese—or American or European—fanatics could place the weapon in the center of any city. The Gang of Four could extend their rule to all the decadent societies of the West. The Gang of Four commanded their scientists to produce the necessary bombs.

After Mao's death, as Wei Ho prepared to attack the world's democracies, popular forces in the Communist Party, enraged by the chaos of the Cultural Revolution, attacked the Gang of Four. Jiang Qing and her clique disappeared into prison. Thousands of their obsequious followers faced firing squads. Pragmatists purged the fanatics, redirected the resources of China to improving the lives of its people. The Peoples' Paradise professed Marxism, yet practiced socialism heavily laced with private enterprise.

Endless interrogation and torture broke the Gang of Four. Before following their lackeys to the execution wall, the members of the clique dictated thousand-page confessions, exposing the shadowy Wei Ho to the light of People's Justice.

Wei Ho fled China with a freight train of gold. He took sanctuary first in Cambodia as the Communist Khmer Rouge decimated their population in their drive to create a Marxist fantasy land. That horror brought economic collapse and nationwide starvation. Seeing the opportunity for quick conquest, the Vietnamese invaded. Wei Ho fled again. With a personal guard of

Cambodian mercenaries, he escaped through Laos to northern Thailand, then to Burma.

He did not forget his plans for world power. In the years of his pupil's marriage to Mao Tse-Tung, when Wei Ho had ruled China through Jiang Qing, his power over the nation had been subtle yet absolute. The old warlord of drugs and prostitution lost the chance to be Emperor of the World only by a factional clash within the Communist Party.

From the mountains of Burma, with tons of gold and a mercenary army, he again plotted nuclear terrorism. His researchers found an unmined and unprotected deposit of uranium in the Andes mountains of Bolivia. His spies in the Free World's atomic industries learned of a brilliant nuclear physicist who suffered from narcotic addiction. Wei Ho's gold bought technicians who would go anywhere, serve any employer. International terrorist groups received word of opportunities for trained, disciplined soldiers.

The Empire of Wei Ho rose from the Amazon.

20

"Holy goddamn," Gadgets swore. "The Atomic Yellow Peril."

Lyons stared out at the moonlit rain forest floating past them, alone with his thoughts. Shirtless, his upper body black with genipap, he wore his gray combat pants to cover the bandage on his piranha wound. Blancanales flicked the rewind switch of the tape unit and listened to snatches of the Stony Man CIA-NSA report. After a few replays, he let Gadgets tape his acknowledgment and outgoing report. Passing the signal through the scrambler, Gadgets transmitted the message in a high-speed screech of electronic noise.

Looking aft, Blancanales checked the river. The patrol boats towed the paddle-wheeler backward downstream. Brazilian farmers in army uniforms manned the helms. If observed from the air, the men and boats would appear to be slaver-commanded.

Hammers rang on sheet metal, power drills whined as the ironsmith and his helpers fabricated boiler-plate armor for the PT boats' gunners. Other men on the paddle-wheeler's cargo deck gave the aluminum dinghies and canoe a last coat of black paint. In the ship's cabins, the Indians caught a few hours' sleep before the assault on the slaver camps.

A hand radio squawked. Gadgets monitored a report to Lieutenant Silveres from the work crew returning with the weapons and cruiser captured from the slavers.

After the Portuguese-speaking settler cut off, the lieutenant translated.

"They have the weapons. They come downstream. No problems."

"At dawn." Lyons finally spoke. "At dawn we hit them. Like this."

Spreading out paper on a table stained by the blood of the captain, Able Team plotted the destruction of Wei Ho.

Only an hour remained until the first gray light of dawn. Mist swirled around the lights of the ancient vessel. Carl Lyons, Pol Blancanales and Gadgets Schwarz stepped from the rail of the paddle-wheeler's cargo decks to the decks of the patrol boats and the captured slaver cruiser.

Gadgets and Blancanales checked the mountings of the heavy weapons on the cruiser, congratulating the workmen on their quick installation. The slavers' cruiser/troop boat now carried two M-60s and two MK-19 40mm full-auto grenade launchers. A group of Brazilian settlers, some of the men army veterans, manned the weapons. Lieutenant Silveres, weak but able to translate, would man the ship's communications, monitoring the slaver transmissions and relaying radio instructions from the assault force to his gunners.

On one of the patrol boats, Lyons moved through the assembled Indian warriors in a last check of their weapons and spirits. They laughed and joked with him, flourishing their Remingtons and G-3s. He counted their bandoliers of 12-gauge shells, mentally calculating their rate of fire versus the ammunition they carried. He knew this would be their heaviest action yet. Then he saw some men packing nylon rucksacks heavy with double-ought shells.

They knew what they were up against, Lyons nodded to himself. No doubt about it.

The black-painted men inspected him also, joking to one another, touching the battle rig Lyons wore. Still shirtless, his body blacked with genipap, he wore all his weapons: the shoulder-holstered Python, the Beretta, the Atchisson slung over his shoulder. Bandoliers crossed his chest, making him look like a Mexican bandit. His radio hung on his Beretta's web belt with magazine pouches. A fragmentation grenade weighed down each thigh pocket. He wore his black-canvas-and-nylon jungle boots, a double-edged fighting knife taped inside his left boot top. He moved slowly with the weight of the weapons, the deck creaking under his boots.

"Boats look good," Gadgets called across to him. He pointed at the black dinghies and canoe bobbing beside the PT boat.

"Tell those farmers one last time," Lyons shouted. "No heroes, no widows. They stay safe. We promised their wives."

Lieutenant Silveres called out to the farmers on the other two patrol boats. Workmen had added steel gunner shields and an extra M-60 to each of the fast fiberglass boats. The men shouted out answers. "They understand."

"Then let's move!"

Motors rumbled, coughing puffs of black diesel soot into the night. Wives and families and friends called out from the rails of the paddle-wheeler and waved as the four river craft pulled away. In a minute, they left the voices and waves of the people far behind.

Lyons keyed his hand radio. "Lieutenant! Call that steamboat, tell them to get it moving. Can't have them anywhere near...."

Even as he spoke, the paddle-wheeler's whistle

shrieked a farewell. The side blades churned the river, taking the families south, where they would wait in concealment for their men to return.

Engine rpm vibrating the river cruiser, Blancanales and Lieutenant Silveres stepped into the cabin. Colonel Gomez sat bound to a chair.

"You will die, stupids," the colonel raved. "The Chinese gang kill you all. Gringos and Indians, stupids."

"To you, traitor," the lieutenant told him, "what happens at dawn does not matter. You will die. Perhaps today, perhaps tomorrow, in front of a firing squad. Perhaps they hang you. You betrayed our country for gold."

The colonel spat at the lieutenant. The wounded young officer paled with anger. He sat down abruptly, for his blood loss had left him weak. Blancanales stepped up to the colonel, slammed the heel of his hand into the prisoner's solar plexus. Doubling over, Colonel Gomez choked and gasped.

Blancanales jerked the colonel's head back by his pomaded hair. "Don't spit. It is not polite. If you follow our instructions, you will live to have a trial. If you try to warn the other mercenaries, we will kill you. It makes no difference to us if you live or die."

Struggling to breathe, his eyes streaming tears, the colonel nodded his head.

Slipping out a knife, Silveres reached for the prisoner. Blancanales caught his hand.

"I do not mean to kill him. But he shames that uniform."

Grasping the insignia on the colonel's fatigue sleeve, Lieutenant Silveres cut the unit patch away. He stripped the fatigues of all rank and unit identification. He threw the bits of cloth and metal to the floor. "Judas. Traitor."

Their wakes white on the black waters of the river, the river craft left the Mamoré and pushed upstream against the slow current of the tributary. The endless rain forest slid past, the masses of high trees deep shadows against the star-shot violet of the infinite night sky. To the east, the sky began to pale.

Lyons paced the deck of the PT boat, turning over in his head every detail of the coming assault. The interrogations of several mercenaries had provided good information on the layout and defenses of the slaver complexes.

The slaver city sprawled along several miles of river, compounds and equipment yards and the reactor sites interconnected by an asphalt all-weather road. In the first complex, Cambodian and Thai mercenaries occupied a compound a hundred yards from the riverbank. They guarded Wei Ho's domed garden and compound, several hundred yards farther inland. An asphalt road connected the two compounds. A mile upstream, there were equipment yards, a narrow airfield, and apartments for the technicians. Another mile upstream, a camp of European and American mercenaries guarded the slave compound.

Three miles of swamp and forest separated the slaves from the first of three atomic reactors, Unit One, gutted by the "accident." The other two Units were miles farther upriver. But the assault force would avoid the atomic reactors. They would attack Wei Ho.

The Indians broke into a sing-song chant. Squatting shoulder to shoulder against the gunwales of the PT boat, they swayed and nodded their heads to the simple rhythm. Lyons leaned against the cabin and scanned the darkness ahead of them. Nothing. He listened to the warriors' song. He asked Thomas, "What is the song you're singing?"

Thomas smiled, shook his head. "Make no sense in English. Very old song."

"Is it a prayer? Like in church?"

"No, only song."

"Tell me. I want to know," Lyons insisted.

"It about women drinking...drinking much and want man to lie down with them...but men drink too much and can't get up...so the women get no love...."

Lyons burst out laughing. "Sure it makes sense in English."

His laugh died. Light glowed on the far shore of the river. Lyons motioned at the Indians. They were silent. He keyed his hand radio. "Wizard. Political. Lieutenant."

Their voices answered. "The city?"

"You got it."

Above Lyons, a hand radio squawked in Portuguese as the lieutenant issued instructions to the helmsman and the two Brazilians who manned the M-60s. The PT boat slowed as the dark form of the river cruiser came up to their side. The hulls bumped. Gadgets and Blancanales stepped down to the smaller boat.

Blancanales waved goodbye to the farmers manning the weapons. He called out to Lieutenant Silveres, *"Vaya con Dios, hermano."*

"Good luck to you, Yankees."

The cruiser and the two other PT boats continued upriver. The helmsman of their boat stayed back. Able Team and their Indian allies watched the river and the distant forest. The Brazilian gunners went to their weapons, waited. Above the river the stars had faded. The eastern sky was turning gray.

The helmsman called down to Able Team in broken Spanish. *"Vamos, gringos. Ahora."*

Veering for the opposite riverbank, the patrol boat cut through darkness and low mist. Lyons signaled

Thomas. Gadgets and Blancanales gave their battle rigs a last pat-down check. Thomas crowded his men against the stern.

Lines of lights, fuzzed by early morning mist, marked a dock. The helmsman kept his distance, dropping the rpm to a whisper and drifted past. Then he eased the throttle open to imperceptibly gain speed.

The drone of a diesel generator carried from the shore. Lyons peered into the chill darkness, watching for the second pier.

"Allá," the helmsman whispered, his voice like a shout to the tensed warriors.

Faint glowing spots emerged from the lightening night. Lyons hand-signaled the others. The PT boat stopped dead in the water as the assault force climbed from the rails. The men lowered themselves into the small boats.

Hands clutched ropes as men fumbled to their places in the dark. Lyons found his seat in a dinghy, felt the tiny boat sway and bob when the last man crowded aboard. Aluminum scraped fiberglass as the men with oars pushed away from the PT boat. The engine chugged again. The hull slipped away in the darkness.

Oars pulled at the black mirror of the river. Mist billowed and swirled. The men rowed quickly, carefully, never splashing, never banging the oars against the boats.

A black rectangle loomed against the gray sky. Pressing themselves low in the boat, the men looked up at the vertical wall of steel containers on a barge. A ray of lighted mist projected from the window of a toolshed on the docks.

Touching the earphone from his hand radio, Lyons keyed his transmit and whispered, "The current's carried us downstream. We might have a hot landing."

"Check," Blancanales answered.

"Maybe," Gadgets acknowledged from the canoe.

The oarsmen kept their strokes steady, silent. Lights on the riverbank made gray mist glow yellow. Lyons scanned the water behind them, caught two shadows sliding over the water: the other dinghy and the canoe.

Sand scraped the aluminum keel. Jamming the oars into the shallow water, the rowers steadied the dinghy as the other men slipped into the water. Lyons dragged his feet through the shallows, not risking a splash. Easing himself prone on the beach, he waited, listening. The other men fanned out around him. Ahead of them, a tangle of reeds stood motionless in the windless pre-dawn.

A truck's engine revved somewhere. The drone of the diesel generator drifted to them from time to time. The second dinghy and the canoe slid onto the beach. Boots and sandals crushed the sand.

Lyons waited until all the movement behind him went still, then crept through the high reeds. He heard grasses swish against moving men. At the top of the riverbank, Lyons and the Xavantes came to raw mud and gravel. Staying low in the reeds, he scanned the cleared ground.

To one side he saw an open-sided steel shelter, only a roof on poles to offer workers a relief from the sun and rain. A single bare incandescent bulb dangled on a wire, insects orbiting the point of brilliance. The light spilled over a wide area surfaced with asphalt and gravel. Lyons keyed his radio. "No go here. A lighted parking lot. Bear to the south. I'll catch up."

Boots scuffed on asphalt. Lyons dropped flat, listened. He heard a mechanical snick. A rifle safety! They'd spotted him!

Ten yards to his side a cigarette lighter flared, the mist glowing for an instant. Lyons parted the reeds to see the ember of a cigarette arc as a sentry took a drag, then let his arm drop.

"We got a merc on guard here," he whispered into his hand radio. "I see only one. I assume there's two. I'm taking them out."

"Do it," Gadgets's voice answered from the tiny jack plugged into Lyons's ear.

First he crept back and found Thomas. Pointing toward the sentry, Lyons held up one finger, two fingers. Thomas nodded. Lyons pointed to Thomas and another man and motioned for them to follow. Then he snaked through the mist-damp reeds, closing in on the sentries. The odor of tobacco drifted in the mist.

They were racing the dawn. Lyons slid his Beretta from the holster and eased back the hammer. He moved on. He felt reeds catching his Atchisson, squeaking slightly as they slid over the plastic. He froze for a moment and listened. Boots paced the asphalt.

Lyons continued. One hand in front of the other, his belly pressed to the matted weeds, he closed distance.

His hand touched a face, the sleeping man's breath catching, his head turning away from Lyons's touch. Lyons scrambled inches forward, sliding his body over the man's head, his body deadening the slap of a slug smashing through a skull. The dead man thrashed for a moment, went slack soon enough. The other sentry still paced the road to the pier.

Easing forward, Lyons stayed flat. He watched the sentry pace and smoke. He waited. The mercenary turned his back. Lyons rose to a crouch and swung up the Beretta.

Headlights swept the reeds as a truck turned onto the pier road. Bouncing over the ruts and broken asphalt, the troop truck bore down on Lyons.

21

Caught in the headlights, Lyons sat back down in the reeds, his legs and boots still out in the open. The sentry turned, blinking against the glare. Blinded, the man turned to Lyons and spoke in Spanish. The truck downshifted, low-geared past Lyons and swung in a wide circle to turn around.

Two mercenaries hopped off the tailgate. Snapping up the Beretta again, Lyons put a single shot into the head of the sentry near him. Then he left the reeds in a sprint, his long legs straining against the weight of the weapons he carried. He fired three-shot bursts into the two mercenaries and then vaulted onto the tailgate.

Lyons was in a tangle of arms and legs; the Beretta's slugs slapped flesh. He kicked and elbowed, fired burst after burst into the mercenaries there. Dropping out an empty magazine, he jammed in another fifteen rounds. He heard steps behind the truck, whipped around, the Beretta on line for a target.

Thomas and three Xavantes were rushing toward and around the truck. Lyons heard a machete strike steel, heard tempered glass pop. A flurry of machete hacks chopped meat in the front seat.

Lyons saw a soldier on the road flop over and grab up a rifle. Snap-sighting, Lyons fired a burst. The slugs slapped the man's head sideways. Other slugs whined into the distance. The soldier still managed to lurch to his knees, shattered jaw and face hanging, and shouldered his rifle. Lyons fired more bursts into the almost-dead soldier's chest and face. The impacts finally knocked him down and out. That one did not want to die.

Keeping the auto-pistol pointed at the bodies sprawled on the truck's floor, Lyons grabbed dead men, dragged them to the tailgate one-handed, the pistol cocked, the safety off. Xavantes grabbed the bodies.

"Thomas!" Lyons called out. "Dump them in the brush. Hide them."

As he reached to grab another dead mercenary, an arm swung up from the floor with a knife. Lyons blocked the arm, fired a burst into a wounded man's face. Flicking the fire selector down to single shot, Lyons put a death-slug into two more palpitating mercenaries. Then he kicked them to make sure.

"Goddamn nine-millimeter!" he cursed. "It's not the right slug for this!"

Blancanales, Gadgets and the Indian warriors dragged the last bodies into concealment.

"Change in plans," Lyons announced. "Same routine but we ride. Yeah?"

"Make it, man," Gadgets agreed. "Full speed ahead."

"Thomas, Gadgets, get all the Indians in the back. Pol, you and me in front. Thomas, keep your radio on. We gonna whip some tricks."

Darting into the reeds, Lyons pulled a fatigue shirt off one of the dead men, then found a floppy hat. He sprinted back to the truck as Blancanales threw it in gear and rolled forward. Stripping off his Atchisson and crisscrossed bandoliers, Lyons put on the mercenary shirt and pulled the hat low over his genipap-blackened face.

Blancanales kept the speed down, following the roads by memory to the main road that connected the several complexes. They paused at the intersection for approaching headlights. A truck came from the direction of the Cambodian garrison. As it passed, they saw Asian faces staring from the interior. Lyons keyed his hand radio. "Lieutenant. This is your beach boy. Things are moving fast. Are you ready?"

"We are ready."

"Is it light yet where you are?"

"A little."

"Stand by. A few more minutes."

Switching off the truck's headlights, Blancanales turned toward the garrison of Wei Ho's personal guards. Gray light defined the forest outline towering above the road. Dawn sky showed through the branches. Watching the odometer, Blancanales called off the distance. "Got to be close now. We go any farther, we risk going straight up to the gates."

"Let's see how this thing does cross-country."

Spotting a dry gap in the trees, Blancanales calmly left the road, low-gearing through the weeds, weaving around stumps, the truck lurching and swaying on its springs. The vehicle smashed through branches, scraped a fender, bumper pushing down saplings. Brush and dead wood scraped the undercarriage. The front wheels dropped into a fern-covered gulley. Blancanales whipped the wheel to the side and stood on the brakes, but too late. The truck slid through ferns and vines, hit bottom.

"End of the line once again," Blancanales laughed as he swung out of the cab.

The truck stood at a forty-five-degree angle in the gulley. Lyons and Blancanales scrambled up the bank, helping the other men from the back. They took a compass bearing and headed for the compound of Wei Ho.

Early morning lighted their way. Birds screeched in the distance. The men slipped through the brush and tangled vines. Insects rose in clouds. Indians with hand radios fanned out in front of the main group.

A point man buzzed Thomas. He translated for Able Team, "Forest ends. There is fence. Then flat land, no trees, nothing."

"The mine field," Blancanales said.

"Can they see the gate?" Lyons asked.

Thomas spoke with his men. "One gate. Many guards."

"That'll be it."

The warriors continued. They joined the point men in the brush at the edge of a gravel road. Across the rutted tracks, an eight-foot chain link fence topped with razor wire kept animals out of a hundred-yard-wide mine field.

An asphalt road fenced on each side with the chain link cut across the open area and headed to the steel gate of the compound. A concrete guardhouse protected the entry. Visible over the high concrete walls was the pleasure dome of the Chinese warlord. The morning's light revealed guards everywhere. Blancanales focused his binoculars on the gate guardhouse.

"Two mercs inside. Cambodians. Two more at the gate. Call Silveres. There can't be any problems."

Lyons keyed his hand radio. "Beach boy calling. You ready?"

"We wait for your word."

"You won't wait much longer." Lyons turned to Blancanales. "Ready?"

"As I'll ever be," Blancanales answered, forcing a smile. He stripped off his pouch of 40mm grenades, then handed his M-16/M-203 to Gadgets. Thomas spoke with one of the warriors as the man stripped off his combat gear.

"They got glass in that bunker," Lyons said to his partners. "We'll put high explosive and one-ounce 12-gauge slugs into them, see if they break. Everyone else puts out cover fire. Thomas, put your snipers up."

The group trotted parallel to the perimeter. Indians with G-3s dropped out, found trees overlooking the compound. Coming to the asphalt lane, other men scrambled up trees to where they would have a line of fire unobstructed by chain link. Blancanales took a G-3 and a Remington and slung the shotgun over his left shoulder. He took frag grenades from his thigh pockets. He straightened the kinks from their cotter pins. He dropped the grenades back in the pockets but did not button the flaps.

Thomas gave the disarmed Indian warrior a length of cord. The man put his hands behind him, looped it around his wrists and held the cord tightly. Blancanales grabbed the free end.

"Wish me luck."

"You got it."

Blancanales gave his Indian "captive" a shove. The prisoner staggered from the roadside brush. Blancanales kicked him in the direction of the gate.

Gadgets and Lyons climbed small trees, went hand over hand through branches until they had firing positions. They lay prone on branches, sighting their weapons: Lyons the Atchisson, Gadgets the M-16/M-203.

Lyons keyed his radio's transmit. "Count down starting, keep the line open."

"The men are at their positions."

"In a minute...."

Kicking his prisoner, jerking on the rope binding his hands, Blancanales drove the Indian toward the gate.

Two Cambodians went to the steel bars that blocked the entry and motioned Blancanales back. Pushing his prisoner onward, the apparent mercenary pointed to the hand radio at his belt and called out, *"Tengo una problema. No lo trabaja.* Problem. Radio. *"¿Comprende usted?"*

The guards unslung their AK-47 rifles and leveled them at the two intruders. Blancanales stopped, backstepped, jerking at the Indian's rope. "No problem. I go! I go!"

Blancanales and the Indian warrior threw themselves into the mud and ruts at the side of the road.

"Now, Lieutenant! Hit them!" Lyons whispered into his hand radio. He sighted the Atchisson on the bulletproof windows a hundred yards away and fired.

The window became a mass of shatters. The two sentries at the gate fired on Blancanales. Rifle fire from high in the trees slammed the Cambodians down.

"One more!" Gadgets shouted from the other tree.

Lyons sighted again, put a second one-ounce steel-cored slug into the window, punched a hole the size of a fist. The M-203 sent a high-explosive grenade arcing for the guardhouse.

It missed the window. Gadgets reloaded as the snipers killed Cambodians running for the gate. A second 40mm grenade arced across the mine field.

White phosphorous turned the concrete guardhouse into a crematorium. Then another high-explosive round hit the gate. But it left the steel unmarked, the gate still closed.

A mile away, a rain of 40mm high-explosive and fragmentation grenades fell on the prefab buildings housing the nuclear technicians. Explosions marched across the apartments. Lines of explosions ripped the equipment yards. Gasoline and diesel fuel flamed. The lieutenant then moved the cruiser upstream, the gunners on the PT boats watching for slaver boats.

Lyons sprinted along the road. Forty-millimeter grenades passed over his head, hit inside the walled compound. Indian snipers in the trees killed every exposed Cambodian. Fire from Blancanales's G-3 slammed a guard's chest, staggered the man off the wall. The Indian at the roadside sighted over his Remington's barrel as he waited for a target.

Throwing himself prone in the mud only twenty feet from the gate, Lyons sighted the Atchisson on the gate's steel bars. But he declined to waste the slug. There was nothing vulnerable. Steel horizontals four inches square braced the bars. Concrete shrouded both ends of the gate. He shouted into his hand radio:

"I'm going over the top!"

"Don't!" Gadgets screamed.

"Only one way in...." Slinging his auto-shotgun over his shoulder, Lyons pulled the fragmentation grenades from his pants' thigh pockets. He jerked out the pins, holding the levers down as he dashed to the concrete wall. He threw the grenades over, one to the right, one to the left, and waited.

Blasts sent thousands of steel razors through the air. Lyons grabbed the bars and climbed and threw a leg over the top. An AK slug shriek-roared past his head. A slug hit steel. The shock went through the steel like hammers to his palms. Then he continued over, dropping to the asphalt, rolling, his Atchisson clattering.

Python now in hand, he scrambled for cover. Slugs from a G-3 at the tree line took out an Asian with an AK. Lyons saw a rifle barrel slide out of a fire port. He put a .357 hollowpoint through the slot. The rifle barrel jerked about, slid back, caught on its front sight.

From a doorway, three Cambodians rushed him.

Double-actioning 158-grain hollowpoints, Lyons put a slug through the chest of the first man before he took two steps. The Asian lurched but continued forward. Other slugs went into the second and third mercenaries, blood and flesh spraying from their backs. They went down. Lyons fired another shot through the first man, saw him fall. Struggling with the twisted sling, Lyons tried to get the Atchisson off his shoulder.

One of the dying mercenaries on the ground raised his rifle. Lyons snapped a shot at the man's face, saw his shoulder spray flesh. The AK pointed and flashed. . . .

Diving, Lyons heard slugs punching concrete. In front of him, a Cambodian stepped away from the wall and brought his AK to line on Lyons's head. Lyons rolled to the side. One-handed, he threw open the Python's cylinder as he slipped a speed-loader from a belt pouch. He pushed the cartridges into the cylinder.

A blast ripped away the guard's head as his finger touched the trigger. Then he thrashed headless on the blacktop, his unfired rifle falling from his hands.

Lyons snapped his Python closed and looked back. Surrounded by swirling black smoke from the guard-house, the Indian "prisoner" dropped from the steel gate, Remington in his hands. He fell in a crouch and fired again. An AK slug slammed him back.

Lyons, twisting his auto-shotgun free, sighted across the asphalt parking area at the bulletproof glass of a guard station, then shattered the glass with a one-ounce slug. He dropped the magazine still containing four slugs into his thigh pocket and jammed in double-ought/number two steel loads.

The Indian staggered to his feet, trying to make it to cover. Another slug hit him, punching into his leg. His leg flew out as if he slipped. Spraying the area with two wild blasts, Lyons dashed to the man and grabbed his wrist and dragged him to the cover of a doorway. Inside, Lyons saw stairs to the walkway on the wall.

With a through-and-through chest wound and a bullet-shattered leg, the Indian reloaded his Remington. Shock glazed his eyes but he still moved. The warrior pointed at the concrete walls of the main house, at the protected guard stations, at the gun ports. He shook his head to Lyons, then motioned to where the others fired from outside for the others to come. Lyons nodded, crept up the stairs leading to the wall, keeping his head down.

A walkway ran along the top of the wall, reinforced concrete protecting defending soldiers chest-high in front. Lyons eased one more step up the stairs. He saw no concrete on the side of the house and dome, only a safety railing. He bobbed his head up above the stairs, saw a fighting position on top of the guardhouse, the walls concrete and four feet high. Smoke swirled.

Between him and the guardhouse, a wounded Cambodian spoke into a walkie-talkie. Lyons dashed to him. Tearing the radio out of the merc's hands, he killed him with a blast to the chest, continued past. Atchisson in one hand, a radio screaming Khmer in the other, Lyons sprinted for the shelter of the concrete and slid in, safe.

Hot concrete scorched his hands and legs. Rising to a crouch, he felt the heat coming through his boots as chemical fire raged inside the guardhouse. Ribbons of smoke came from around the roof hatch.

Lyons saw another hatch. He touched it, found it cool. He pointed his Atchisson down and jerked the hatch open.

The motors for the steel gate! Lyons went down a utility ladder. He searched for a breaker box, found it. Chinese ideograms and incomprehensible printing labeled the switches. He threw all the switches. An electric motor whined.

His hand radio buzzed even as he reached for it. "You got it—it's opening. Where are you now?"

"Inside. Your turn."

"Moving!"

Returning to the top of the wall, Lyons lay prone, sighting on rifle ports and guard stations, firing blast after blast. Cambodians and Thais and Chinese died or took cover.

American warriors—Brazilian Indians and Yankee commandos—rushed through the open gate, to besiege the Asians inside the fortress of Wei Ho.

22

Reflecting the hues of the dawn, a column of smoke towered above the jungle. A mile south of Wei Ho's fortress, gasoline exploding in the equipment yard sent balls of flame churning into the smoke. Sheet metal drifted in the smoke and flames like ashes.

Blancanales took his M-16/M-203 over-and-under from Gadgets and loaded a high-explosive 40mm grenade. With the firefight roaring around them, Gadgets shouted into his hand radio, "Wild man! We're in. Where...."

A shadow dropped from the wall. Lyons landed in a crouch beside them. Gadgets stared for an instant. Lyons took the slaver-band walkie-talkie out of his thigh pocket.

"You are one surprising dude!" Gadgets shouted over the noise. He took the radio and lifted it to his ear and switched it on. Voices jabbered back and forth. Gadgets held the radio close to Blancanales. "You understand that?"

"Some of it's Chinese. Don't understand any of it."

"What can you do with the radio?" Lyons asked. "Anything interesting?"

Gadgets grinned. He keyed the transmit. "Chinese Commie doper punks! You die! We come to kill that old pimp!"

Lyons laughed, shook his head. "Get serious...."

"Serious isn't fun." Gadgets found a spent shotgun

casing on the asphalt. He flattened the cardboard tube
and jammed it under the transmit key. "Long as the
battery lasts, they got to talk over all this noise.... Say
your prayers, Commies! We come to kill you!" Gadgets
set the radio in the open, the microphone turned away
from them.

"Straight in," Blancanales told Lyons. He pointed at
a sheet steel door. An AK fired from the shattered glass
of the not-so-bulletproof port.

"If we can...." Lyons dropped out his Atchisson's
magazine and slipped in a half-spent mag, of heavy
slugs.

Blancanales scanned the interior of the compound.
From cover, Indian warriors aimed fire into the rifle
ports and windows. Few AKs answered. He shouldered
his assault rifle/grenade launcher. "One in the window."

High explosive threw glass and debris out the guard
station's port. No fire came now. Lyons sighted on the
sheet steel door, punched a ragged hole through it with
a high-velocity one-ounce slug. He sighted again,
squeezed the trigger so slowly....

The hole became a rip. Lyons sighted higher, spread
the rip another two inches. Blancanales sighted his
grenade launcher. He fired. The blast slammed a vast
dent into the steel, tearing the steel open. A head-sized
hole yawned in the security door.

"I'm rushing it," Blancanales told them, passing
Gadgets his weapon. He checked the two fragmentation
grenades in his thigh pockets and pointed out his path
across the asphalt. "I'll cut to the side, you two put
some fire out, I'll put frags in there. You two follow.
Got it?"

Lyons and Gadgets nodded. Lyons fired the last slug
in the magazine straight through the hole, then jammed

in a full box mag. Gadgets slipped out another magazine for his CAR-15 and held it ready.

Zigzagging, Blancanales sprinted for the steel door as his partners fired burst after burst at the rifle positions. He ran without slowing and slammed his shoulder into the concrete. Pulling the pin out of a grenade, he let the lever fly free, waited for the count of four, heaved it through the ripped steel door. Dust and smoke blasted out as he turned away, covering his head. Then Blancanales stepped across to the guard station. He dropped in the second grenade. Debris flew from the interior.

Gadgets covered Lyons. Soon he followed, also. Against the concrete wall of the fortress-house, none of the AK fire could touch them. The Indian gunners still fired at guard ports around the house. Gadgets returned Blancanales's weapon and the few remaining 40mm grenades. He took out the two hand grenades he carried and pulled the pin of one.

Waving his arms to the Indians, Gadgets sidestepped. The gunners held their fire as Gadgets slipped up to a shattered port and let the lever fly. After four seconds, he slammed it in. The blast silenced the rifleman inside. Gadgets dashed to the other rifle port, silenced it also.

Indians rushed across the asphalt. They crowded around the entry. Two warriors climbed through the shattered port and called out to the others. Several men followed. Thomas shouted to Able Team, "Inside door open, come!"

Fire from an AK hammered the steel. An Indian was slammed back. Lyons put his Atchisson through the hole in the steel. He sighted on an Asian at the end of the corridor. Steel shot tore a nine-inch wide hole in the Asian's chest.

Gadgets and Blancanales climbed up, got swept along in a charge, Indians firing shotguns continuously, men crouching down to reload, letting the others surge forward.

A grenade bounced from the guard station. Gadgets kicked it back, screamed to the others, dropped flat. Indians tripped over him, sprawling. Other men crouched as the grenade skittered to the end of the entry corridor. It spun like a top for an instant and came to rest against the security door.

The corpse of a Cambodian took most of the shrapnel and blast. A few steel razors slashed men's backs, peppering prone men with wounds. Bloody, they still rushed forward again. An Indian fired wild into the guard position, then pumped the Remington's action and fired again. A torn body flopped out. Blancanales rushed forward to strip three grenades from the guard's pockets. Gadgets found the door's power switch and hit it.

"Throw those grenades! Now, now, now!"

Blancanales jerked the pins out, lobbed a grenade, pulled another pin, threw that grenade hard. The blasts slammed the interior, one-two, one near the door, the second across the garden. Blancanales pulled the third pin. He snapped his head out for an instant.

He almost lost it. A burst of AK fire came from behind him. He whipped his head back in, bounced the grenade in that direction. He found one of his 40mm buckshot rounds and loaded his grenade launcher. Then he changed the magazine on the M-16.

"Don't!" Gadgets had found another grenade on a second dead merc, and he passed it to his partner.

Lyons charged up behind the attacking force, saw Blancanales let the grenade's lever flip free, count, then toss the frag. An instant after the blast, he dived through the door and rolled across flowers.

A tiny Chinese girl with an Uzi ran at him, her silk

robe fluttering. Blancanales lifted his weapon. Simultaneous blasts from three Remingtons sheared away the upper half of her body.

Slugs from an AK hit the Indians, a warrior dropped, Blancanales spun, saw the shoulder and head of a man holding an auto-rifle. Firing the M-203, Blancanales saw the rifle and arms and head disappear in a spray of gore.

Remingtons and G-3s fired in one continuous roar as the Indians riddled the carved wooden partitions and painted screens inside Wei Ho's palace. Double-ought blasts ripped gaping holes through doors, walls, priceless Chinese art.

Able Team searched for Wei Ho. They killed everything that moved. A boy wearing a girl's gown and makeup ran from hiding, took a burst from an Indian through the back. Serving maids attempted a last desperate defense of their master with the AKs of dead guards. They died.

Lyons kicked a door as slugs punched through the wood. Spinning aside, he ran a few steps, slammed his shoulder against the wall. The carved partition crashed inward, knocking two Chinese guards to the floor. Lyons waved a burst of steel shot over them, their bodies suddenly masses of torn flesh and spilled guts. He saw the old man.

Wei Ho wore a gray English suit cut in the style of the thirties, his thin gray hair combed flat on his skull like a bank clerk. Rimless spectacles perched on the bridge of his fine-boned nose. He sat at a lacquered table, papers and blueprints spread before him.

"Would you kill a defenseless old man?" Wei Ho asked, his whine accented with the preciseness of British schooling.

Lyons brought up the Atchisson even as the old man's

clawlike hand flashed. Dropping low, Lyons saw darts shoot over his head. He decided not to give the warlord another instant of life. He triggered an auto-burst of steel high-velocity shot through the ancient body. The three blasts ripped the old dart-wielder in two.

Rushing in, Blancanales saw the blank-eyed torso and arms drop to the floor, thrash for an instant, blood turning the conservative English suit's fabric to black. Lyons stared down at the dead Chinese. How could a frail old man contain so much evil as Wei Ho did?

"I think you killed him, Lyons. Now move it. We gotta hold this place until the cavalry arrives." Blancanales lifted his hand radio to his mouth. "Gadgets, he's dead. Lieutenant Silveres. Lieutenant! Send out the calls."

On the river cruiser, as the gunners on the deck continued raining high-explosive grenades on the mercenaries, Lieutenant Silveres pressed the transmit button of the long-distance radio, having been briefed by Gadgets on its workings, and sent a high-speed taped message by satellite to American stations in Bolivia, Peru, Washington, D.C., and Virginia.

Then he changed frequencies to radio his commander in the nation's capital of Brasília.

"Men of the American Phoenix have torn into the heart of a great sickness. I was with them. We live. It is great to live! It is great to be here at this victory, greater than you will ever know! Allow me this moment of glory with these men. Then I return. But such men as these will never leave me in spirit. I salute them in your name.

"These damn Yankees...!"

ABLE TEAM

AN EXECUTIONER SERIES

#5 Cairo Countdown

MORE GREAT ACTION COMING SOON!

The U.S. maintained a covert air-force base in Egypt. It operated right out of Cairo's international airport.

Now a terrorist rampage threatened to reveal this sensitive presence in one of the world's top hot spots. No known intelligence agency can risk exposure in order to smash the attack on America's big secret. In the name of the President, and of Mack Bolan—come in, Able!

Watch for new Able Team titles wherever paperbacks are sold.